Birch Hollow
Schoolmarm

Books by Carrie Bender

Miriam's Journal
A Fruitful Vine
A Winding Path
A Joyous Heart
A Treasured Friendship
A Golden Sunbeam

Dora's Diary
Birch Hollow Schoolmarm

Whispering Brook Series
Whispering Brook Farm
Summerville Days
Chestnut Ridge Acres

Miriam's Cookbook

Dora's Diary
1

Birch Hollow Schoolmarm

Carrie Bender

Herald
Press

Scottdale, Pennsylvania
Waterloo, Ontario

Library of Congress Cataloging-in-Publication Data
Bender, Carrie, date.
  Birch Hollow Schoolmarm / Carrie Bender.
    p. cm. — (Dora's diary ; 1)
  ISBN 0-8361-9095-5 (alk. paper)
  1. Amish—Pennsylvania—Fiction. 2. Amish—Minnesota—
    Fiction.
  I. Title. II. Series: Bender, Carrie, date. Dora's diary ; 1.
PS3552.E53845B57 1999
813'.54—dc21   98-50568

F
BEN

The paper in this publication is recycled and meets the minimum requirements of American National Standard for Information Sciences—Permanence of Paper for Printed Library Materials, ANSI Z39.48-1984.

Except as otherwise noted, Scripture is based on the *King James Version of the Holy Bible*, with some adaptation to current English usage. Other credits are listed at the back of the book.

This story is a work of fiction but true to Amish life. Any resemblance to persons living or dead is purely coincidental.

BIRCH HOLLOW SCHOOLMARM
Copyright © 1999 by Herald Press, Scottdale, Pa. 15683
    Published simultaneously in Canada by Herald Press,
    Waterloo, Ont. N2L 6H7. All rights reserved
Web site for Herald Press: www.mph.org
Library of Congress Catalog Number: 98-50568
International Standard Book Number: 0-8361-9095-5
Printed in the United States of America
Cover art and illustrations by Joy Dunn Keenan
Book design by Paula Johnson and Merrill R. Miller

08 09 06 05 04 03 02 01 00 99 10 9 8 7 6 5 4 3 2 1

Contents

Dreams and Schemes

April 10

Dear Diary,

Here I am, upstairs in my room, with sounds of the soft spring evening drifting in through the open window. A robin is singing sweetly from the old apple tree, and a pair of turtledoves are cooing from their perch on the wash line. Neighbor Eli's lambs are baaing from their meadow.

The warm breeze floating in the window is laden with the scent of green grass and freshly plowed fields. A mellow dusk is descending over the countryside, softly, sweetly, peacefully. Ah, springtime, surely it must be the sweetest time of the year, when all nature is awakened and renewed.

I am feeling happy and excited because today is my sixteenth birthday. A whole new era is opening before me. I've finally reached the right age for *rum-schpringing!* (running around with the youths). In one way I can hardly wait to attend my first singing, on Sunday evening. In another way I feel half frightened, wanting to be a little girl again, turning around and hiding behind *Mamm's* (Mom's) skirts. Sigh!

I wonder, *Will I ever get this brand-new diary filled?*

I'm enthusiastic now about keeping a journal, but will it last, or will I toss this in the wastebasket after a few weeks? We'll see.

Maybe starting a new journal like this (something I never did before) will help me in sorting out my feelings and thoughts. I want to write down my goals and dreams for the future.

This evening Mamm and *Daed* (my adoptive parents, Miriam and Nate), and my brothers, Peter and Crist, have gone to visit Grandpa Daves. Younger sister Sadie is curled up on her bed across the hall, reading the *Young Companion* magazine. Just now I took a good look at myself in the mirror and asked myself, "Dora Kauffman, are you really and truly mature enough and fit to begin *rumschpringing*?"

The girl in the mirror stared back at me. She had an oval-shaped face, olive-tinted skin, dark hair and eyes, and she smiled a satisfied smile. Oh dear, I hope I'm not becoming vain or (perish the thought!) haughty. I wouldn't want others to say of me, "She's pretty and she knows it."

I'll try to be as humble and modest as any mother could wish. Mamm has often told me, "Remember, Dora, beauty is only skin deep. It's the inner beauty in the heart that counts in God's sight. As Solomon says, 'Favor is deceitful, and beauty is vain; but a woman that fears the Lord, she shall be praised.' Our faith is more important than looks."

I must confess that what I see inside doesn't please me much. My desire is to grow up to be a good woman, virtuous and beautiful. But, alas, I fear

I am still so immature and have a far way to go till I'm a model of submission and virtue and patience.

Sometimes I wonder whether I'll ever overcome my self-will and my selfish, impatient nature. And I have only four or so years yet in which to do that! I've heard that by the time you are twenty or twenty-one, your character is formed for life. Do I really have only a few more years, and then my personality is set for the rest of my life?

That thought frightens me and makes me want to do all I can to be noble, good, and true. But I do so want to have a good time while I am *rumschpringing*.

Another reason I am happy and excited tonight is because I got another birthday card from Gideon in the mail today! In the eighth grade on Valentine's Day, he gave me a pretty homemade Valentine card with a cute verse written on it.

This isn't the first birthday card he sent me, either, but the one I got from him today was bigger and prettier than ever. Ah—it's getting better! The verses get a little more personal each time.

I'm glad I was the one to bring in the mail so I could slip that envelope under my apron. Mamm and Daed won't need to know. Gideon has been *rumschpringing* for a year already. And now that I'm starting— . . . *ach mei* (oh my), I'd better not count my chicks before they hatch. There are a lot of things that could happen yet.

Oh, there's the rattle of carriage wheels on the lane. Daed and Mamm and the boys are back, and I must go. Good night!

Here I am, back again after a day of hard work, weeding the berry patch. It sure feels good to relax. I see that on Saturday I was so taken up with writing about Gideon that I never got around to telling about my day—my birthday!

At the breakfast table, the whole family sang, "Happy Birthday" to me, and Daed commented, "How fast you are growing up!"

But I'm already grown up, I think.

Peter pulled my ears sixteen times, once for each year of my age.

Mamm gave me a wrapped package. Inside was this brand-new journal, ready for me to write in it. She encouraged me to fill it, and I think I just might. One nice thing about a journal is that you don't have to start at January 1 and you don't have to write every day—just whenever you feel like it. If you tire of it, you can lay it aside for half a year.

Several times I tried to keep a diary with printed dates and a standard space for each day. But then I forgot to write in it for a week or so. Seeing all those empty lines discouraged me, and I gave it up. Now I can put my own dates down each time I get around to writing. Any day, I can write as much or as little as I feel like doing. And I won't leave blank pages! I can still call it a diary if I want to.

Then that evening at the supper table, Little Crist—as we still affectionately call him sometimes even though he is already twelve years old, but small for his age—handed me a small package across the table. It was wrapped in leftover Christmas wrap, and he had even put a bow on top.

I beamed a bright smile at him and said, "*Danki, danki* (thanks), how nice of you!" I thought he looked a bit guilty but couldn't figure out why.

With a grin and dancing eyes, he warned, "Don't open your birthday surprise until after supper!"

When I saw little holes poked in all around the package, I became suspicious. I knew of Crist's tricks and suspected it might be a wrapped lizard or caterpillar. So I laid it aside, pretending innocence.

In honor of my birthday, Mamm had made all my favorite foods—a big platter heaped high with fried chicken legs, steaming mashed potatoes, creamed corn, and cabbage slaw. For dessert we had home-turned vanilla ice cream.

Sadie carried in a cake she had made with sixteen lighted candles on it. She had heaped on lots of pink icing, so that one side was a bit lopsided, and had decorated it with gumdrops. It was delicious!

I told Sadie, "Since you're good enough to make me a cake, I'll let you open my package from Crist."

Crist the *Schnickelfritz* (mischievous child) objected: "No, no, you have to open your own present. It's *your* birthday."

I decided to let him have his fun and proceeded to carefully open the package. Inside was a tiny box. When I lifted the lid, I squealed in mock alarm, just to gratify him. Nestled inside on a bit of straw were four cute little pink baby mice.

I'm not afraid of mice (I'm just glad it wasn't a

big green juicy tobacco worm). But I pretended to be scared and jumped away from the table. Mamm made a fuss and ordered him, "Go right out *right now* and dispose of them properly!"

Such a dear funny family! I feel blessed to have each one of them. Not long after supper, Priscilla (my birth mother) and Henry and their children came over with a gift for me—a dresser set (brush, comb, and mirror) and yarn to make a buggy afghan. They are my second family, nearly as beloved and close to my heart as this household.

Yes, I do feel so happy and blessed these days. I wonder how much Gideon's card has to do with this feeling. What would Mamm and Daed say if they knew? I'm afraid they wouldn't be happy about it, for I've been hearing a few things about Gideon of late. Maybe he's not the tame young boy he used to be.

April 13
.... Brrrr! Springtime weather is so changeable. Just now it feels like winter has come back. This cold snap is supposed to last awhile. The paper says it will be even colder over the weekend.

Mamm, Sadie, and I finished the spring house-cleaning today. All the time I was scrubbing walls, woodwork, and windows, I was polishing my lofty dreams and ideals in my mind—my secret plans for the future.

I daydreamed of having a husband. But try as I

might, I could not make Gideon fit into the picture. My man was just a faceless, nameless figure, but good and loving and kind, dependable as well, and a tower of strength in our dream home.

There would be plenty of sweet babies, a house full of beautiful, healthy children—at least five girls and five boys. They would all be models of perfection, well disciplined and trained. I would be the perfect wife and mother, wise and good, with a kind word of encouragement for everyone.

My dream home would be a bit of heaven on earth, where nary a note of discord ever entered and everyone was happy and good. On and on I rambled in my mind, building castles in the air. . . . My children would never fight. I'd have such a firm, loving way of parenting them that any spats would dissolve before they erupted. My husband and children would adore me and rise up to call me blessed.

The spirit of love and kindness would warm all who entered our home There would always be plenty of money, enough to help others in hard times. No one who needed help would be turned away. No one in our household would ever be sick or have any disability, no one ever sad.

Our prosperous and scenic farm would be the most well kept in the neighborhood. I would be a woman of great wisdom and piety, lovable and beloved by all, a great joy and blessing to others.

Yes, in my lofty daydreams, I was noble and exalted. But, alas, in real life I'm a far cry from sainthood. Just today I fought with Sadie over who gets the nicest dress material from what Mamm brought home. And I scrapped with Peter over who has to wash the *Dachwegli* (carriage) and argued with Crist over a mere trifle.

Sometimes I despair of ever being better. My good resolutions never last long. So soon my sharp tongue and quick temper and self-centeredness take over. I don't love to pray and read the Bible as I should.

Ya, well (yes, well), I've been sitting here on the cedar chest for the past fifteen minutes, staring sadly into space and wishing I could be as good and noble as in my dreams. But just wishing will get me nowhere.

Outside my window a pair of robins have been busy building a nest. Now their day's work is over, and they're both singing so joyously, as if bursting with praise for their Creator. Oh dear, there's Mamm down in the garden with her hoe, planting something. I should be out there helping her instead of sitting here.

April 15
....
Sunday's coming closer, and I'm getting excited and anxious about my first singing. I'm wondering if Gideon will be there—I haven't seen him for a while.

Well, dear diary, today I had a very enjoyable time! I spent the afternoon plowing a field on a sulky (riding) plow, after Daed had struck out starting furrows for several strips of land. Now the plowing is finished.

Peter is still in school, and Daeds (Mamm and Daed) had planned to go to a frolic, so I begged for him to let me finish plowing the last field. Since it looked like rain would be coming by evening, he agreed. He did want that plowing done. I'm sure glad he trusted me with the team. Tonight a spring rain is falling.

I decided I'd show him that I can plow as straight a furrow as any man, and it did go well. Daed even had a word of praise for me at the supper table. It was a satisfying feeling.

Working outside is much more fun than sitting at a quilt, making poky little stitches and pricking my fingers, or standing over a hot stove and cooking. For awhile there, I was wishing I'd have been born a boy. Oh well, there's plenty of time later to be a prim and proper lady.

I was sitting there on the sulky plow seat, behind the great plodding workhorses, with rich black earth being turned up behind me. Mellow blue-gray skies were overhead. I heard the cries of seagulls as they followed the plow, searching for earthworms and grubs. Soft green was coming out on the trees along the creek.

It was all so peaceful and uplifting. I had plenty of time to think of things like joining church and *rumschpringing*. I do so much want to have a fun time!

Monday evening, and it wasn't even a blue Monday for me even though I was out late last night. Now hear this, dear diary: I attended my first singing! At last I'm old enough to enter the thrilling world of *rumschpringing*. Before the evening was over, there was a little too much excitement for even me! I have so much to write about.

First of all, Gideon was not there, but I didn't see any boy who was better looking than he. I keep thinking, *What a fine-looking couple we would make, Gideon and I.* But Mamm keeps saying, "Don't set your cap for Gideon or anyone else. You're much too young to be serious. Anyhow, puppy love usually wags its tail and runs away."

Oh well, thinking about it is exciting, and I guess it won't do any harm.

I wish I'd have an older brother to take me to the singings. Going with a neighbor boy is second best. I traveled with neighbor Eli's Dan and his sister Rachel, and he drives quite a horse. Wow! I wish Daed would have a road horse like that instead of his slow and steady old Dobbin.

Dan's steed was a prancing high-stepper named Rowdy, real upheaded and handsome, a saddlebred with more style and show than the average horse. I loved his pace. He was skittery, too, and there was never a dull moment. Dan had his hands full with him all right. It was a thrilling ride.

The setting sun was spreading a rosy glow in the west and decorating the countryside. Since it was chilly, we snuggled under the carriage robe. I was about as happy and excited as could be. But after a while my leg began to ache where Rachel was sitting on it. She sat on one of my knees and on one of Dan's. They had taken out the back seat to be reupholstered, and we were used to traveling three on a seat, anyhow.

By the time we arrived at the house for the singing, my leg was quite numb. When Rachel got off, it felt as if there were a thousand pinpricks stinging it. When I gingerly got out, my leg gave way. The next thing I knew, I was hobbling and staggering about.

Rachel grabbed my arm and cried, "*Was is letz* (what's wrong)?"

"*Mei Beh iss eigschlofe* (my leg has fallen asleep)."

It was my most embarrassing moment. The boys standing by the barn began to snicker. I was horrified, but Rachel broke into a giggling fit and said, "You're sure to attract a lot of attention, as usual."

We went into the *Kesselhaus* (kettle house) attached to the kitchen and were greeted by a group of laughing, chattering girls. I was glad they hadn't seen me staggering about. We tied our bonnets to a string stretched from one wall to another, beside all the other bonnets.

Rachel and I decided to go into the kitchen right away and find ourselves good seats before the boys came in to sing. In a shadowy corner, we were lucky enough to find a deep windowsill not yet occupied. Sitting there, we could see everything but not be very noticeable ourselves, since we weren't close to the gaslights.

The north end of the kitchen was filling up with girls. Soon the porch door opened, and the boys filed in. I was terribly disappointed that Gideon wasn't among them. It wonders me so why he wasn't there. I hope he didn't break a leg or something worse.

Rachel whispered to me, "See that third boy on the bench by the door? That's Benny Byler. He just came into our district to work for one of his uncles and will be *rumschpringing* with our group."

"You mean the one with the crooked nose?"

She nodded. "He was hit by a baseball at school when he was in the eighth grade. His nose was broken, but otherwise he's real good-looking."

"Yes, he is handsome," I whispered. He had wavy dark-brown hair and a nice profile. I couldn't help but tease Rachel a little: "You seem awfully interested in him. I think you'd make a nice couple."

She covered her face with her hands, as though to cover a blush, and giggled. "Would we? I am awfully interested in him, but I think I'd better leave him for you, the way he's giving you the eye."

I poked her with my elbow for that!

When the singing started, it gave me a joyous and uplifted feeling to hear the blending of the boys' and girls' voices in the dear old hymns. The music was even echoing off the ceiling. When the parting hymn was announced, *es hot mich so geschpitt* (it spited me so) that it was over.

Then wham! Something hit me on the cheek.

Whiz! Something else just missed my nose. The boys were throwing candy!

"Wow!" Rachel exclaimed. "The boys really are noticing you. I guess it's their way of welcoming you to the singing. Benny threw that last piece, maybe both pieces. He's probably wondering who the *schee Maedel* (pretty girl) is."

"Ach, stop it," I said, giggling. "He's probably aiming for you, anyway."

"Oh no," Rachel objected. "I haven't a sliver of a chance if he wants you."

Hmmm!

A group of girls started a party game. That's when the rest of the boys came in, the ones who had been hanging around outside during the singing. Again I was disappointed to see that Gideon wasn't among them. I wouldn't mind—

April 20

.... Maybe I can finish my story now. Last evening I was rudely interrupted by Sadie calling up the stairs, "*De Geil sin aus! De Geil sin aus!* (the horses are out). *Kumm dapper!* (come quick) and help chase them in."

There they were, with heads up high, galloping out the field lane, free as birds. Their tails and manes were flying in the wind. We had a merry chase from one end of the field to the other. Finally we got them herded in.

Crist had forgotten to close the feedlot gate after

letting the cows into the meadow. After I came back to my room, I was too tired to write another word. Now I don't remember how I was going to finish that last sentence anyway. But I must write about the experience we had on the way home from the singing.

It had gotten chillier. Dan remarked, "We're in for another killing frost by morning, but in my carriage, we'll be as snug as a bug in a rug." He reached down and flipped a switch. "With me, you'll ride in style! No frozen toes and fingers in the winter weather, and no need for carriage robes in spring and fall."

He explained why. "I've installed a propane gas heater. It even has a fan, run from the carriage battery. That'll blow the heat across our toes."

"This is fit for a queen," I told him. "The girls will be falling over each other for the chance to ride with you."

He smiled and said, "At your service, ma'am."

Now what did he mean by that?

A pleasant warmth began to fill the carriage. We were riding in the lap of luxury. This time it was my turn to sit on top, and if a leg fell asleep, it wouldn't be mine. The robe wasn't needed, so I shoved it under the seat.

We hadn't gone far when Dan suddenly called out, "What's that?" He quickly opened the storm-front window. Rowdy reared up high, and Rachel screamed. Dan yanked open the *Schiewer* (sliding carriage door) and got out.

Somebody had rolled a telephone pole across the

road. What a mean trick! It could have caused a bad accident. Dan handed the reins to me, since I was on top, and rolled the pole off the road. All the while, Rowdy was prancing nervously. In a few minutes, we were on our way again, and he just wanted to gallop.

Dan opened the *Schiewer* to speak to him and calm him. Then we all smelled smoke.

Rachel said, "I don't see a bonfire anywhere."

There was a crackling sound from under the seat, and a wisp of smoke curled upward from it. Rachel yelled, "Help! Fire! Fire!"

Dan pulled the carriage robe forward, and a small flame leapt upward from it. We all tried to stamp it out. But another flame took its place, and then another. The wooden floor itself was burning. Dan yelled, "Jump out quick before your dresses catch fire."

We both jumped. It wasn't long before Dan had to jump, too. Rowdy was going crazy, and it was all Dan could do to keep him under control. We girls watched in helpless horror as the flames took hold, then leapt higher and higher. The whole carriage was engulfed in a pillar of fire that stabbed through the darkness.

Then, thankfully, help arrived. It was Benny Byler on a scooter. I was never so glad to see a crooked nose before. He sprang into action and helped to unhitch Rowdy. When Dan led him away, he was none the worse for it, except for a singed tail.

Soon the carriage was only a heap of glowing

orange embers and metal scraps. Luckily it was off the road, due to Rowdy's antics. Some more boys arrived on the scene, and Benny told us, "Girls, wait here and I'll bring my rig and take you home." He did just that.

Dan muttered, "I guess I needed a metal shield between the heater and the floor." Then he hoisted himself onto Rowdy and rode him home. What a relief that no one was hurt, except for minor burns and bruises!

Since then I've been pondering Benny's friendliness and helpfulness. Was he only doing it as his Christian duty, or was there another reason? I wouldn't be a bit surprised if he's interested in Rachel. But on the other hand, what boy wouldn't want to rescue girls who had been in a burning carriage.

Of course he took pity on us and offered to drive us home when he saw there was nothing left of the *Dachwegli* but scraps and ashes. It probably wasn't more than common courtesy. He would have been mighty hard-hearted not to offer it. But he *was* extra nice. Now if it wouldn't be for Gideon . . .

April 21

Well, well, I'm surprising myself by writing in my diary nearly every day. I suppose it will wear off after awhile. This was a lovely spring day, balmy and pleasant after the cold snap we had over the weekend.

I spent the day helping Priscilla—a job I love even though I don't get paid for it. She has three prison babies again. With her own three, that makes quite a houseful. Children's Services places those extra babies with her. Their mothers are in prison.

The three she has just now are from one family, and they're quite dark-skinned and cute as can be. Courtney is two and a half, with a head full of tightly curled black hair and a wide smile. Billy is one and a half. His head looks shaved, and his cheeks are fat. The baby, Kaylee, is only three months old but is already bright eyed and smiles a lot.

Their mother is only nineteen, and she is a drug addict. I doubt that they even have a dad who claims them. Poor, poor babies. It doesn't seem fair at all. What have they done to deserve such a mother? What hope is there for their future?

They're so dear and sweet, so defenseless and lovable. Priscilla has her hands full caring for them all, but her own girls, Miriam Joy and Bathsheba, are already a big help to her. They are good young babysitters, indeed.

I'm really quite tired tonight, but it's such a satisfying kind of tiredness—a day well spent. Priscilla said that she keeps thinking that if the babies stay long enough, she will be able to tell them many Bible stories. Then maybe they will grow up to be good persons who love Jesus, can live for the Lord, and belong to the kingdom of heaven. She can't bear to think otherwise. Neither can I.

Peter had a sad and frightening experience today. A month or so ago, Daed bought him a beautiful high-stepping Hackney pony, after over a year of coaxing from Peter. He would cut out ads from the farm paper and show them to Daed. At every horse sale, Peter watched for one.

Finally he got his wish. He named the pony Lightning. It was his pride and joy. I don't believe there ever was a pony that received more attention and better care than Lightning.

Then today after school, Daed sent Peter with his pony and little spring wagon for a bag of horse feed. On the way to the mill, they were crossing the highway on a green light when a drunk driver hit them.

I shudder to think what might have happened if the car would've had more speed! As it was, the wagon was smashed and Lightning tore loose and galloped down the highway and into an oncoming car. He crashed into the windshield, showering the driver with broken glass. The impact killed the pony.

Thankfully, the driver wasn't hurt except for minor cuts. Peter picked himself up off the road. Besides being scratched and scuffed up, he wasn't hurt either. The drunk was arrested, and a policeman brought Peter home.

Daed told him, "The pony can be replaced." But Peter could not accept the loss and went to bed without eating supper. I don't blame him a bit for being shook up. The roads are dangerous enough these days even when drivers are sober.

May 3

.... Last night I attended my second singing. This time Gideon was present. No crooked nose for him! He was the most handsome boy there by far. I was glad I had spent as much time as I did in front of the mirror, preening and primping. I had made sure that every hair was in place and the bow of my *Kapp* (head covering) strings was tied just right.

Gideon wasn't in the house for the singing part of the evening. But when the party games began, he was right there in the center of the whirl. Time and again, his eyes beckoned me to join in the activity, but I couldn't quite muster up the spunk. Next time I will!

Rachel was called outside, and I was all excited. Later I asked her, "Was that Benny Byler?"

She burst out laughing good-naturedly and said, "Benny's my first cousin! That's why I'm leaving him for you."

Hmmm . . . I just won't let her teasing go to my head.

Dan already has another carriage, but I don't think he'll get a new propane heater for it next winter. He said he thinks the head of the old heater fell off when Rowdy acted up. *Ya well*, I gotta go.

May 6

.... Outside, everything has turned so wondrously green, the grass in the meadows and the leaves in the trees. The garden things are growing almost like Jack's beanstalk. It's truly an awe-inspiring miracle after the drab browns and gray of winter. We had a warm spring rain and everything, even the weeds, are lush and green.

Spring makes the heart sing! I long to have wings like a bird to soar over the countryside, taking in all the springtime beauties so fresh with sweet fragrance.

Daed put up a purple martin house this spring, and now several pairs of them have set up housekeeping in it. I love to hear their cheerful warbling and gurgling as they "talk" to each other and gracefully swoop and soar around their new home. They're really useful birds, too. They eat a lot of harmful insects and bugs in the garden.

Tonight when I was out spading a flowerbed, a *Dachwegli* drove in. Preacher Emanuel and his wife were coming to borrow a tool from Daed.

Emanuel's wife called out to me, "*Wie geht's rumschpringing* (how does it go, running around with the youths)?"

I answered, "Great!" And I meant it, too. So far it has been just great. I'm glad this isn't yet the time for me to join the church. I'm certainly not ready yet. My head is so full of frivolous thoughts and *rumschpringing*. About all I can think of is having a good time. I hope *der Gute Mann* (the Good One, God) will understand.

Lilac blossom time! My favorite time of year. We have two bushes of the old-fashioned kind, lavender and white. They are the most sweetly fragrant imaginable.

I brought a huge bouquet in, and it perfumes the whole kitchen. The fire in the range is out, so I covered it with a piece of new oilcloth and set the vase of lilacs on top. It makes a pretty picture.

I love to go for the cows these days. The meadows are absolutely delightful in the early morning. I wish I'd have words to describe the scene. It's so lovely, sweet, and fragrant, with buttercups in the lush green grass, heavy with dew. I see and sniff the sweet-scented wild cherry blossoms and hear the chorus of the singing birds. My senses are so overloaded that I almost swoon with joy.

Now the news: Rachel and I were invited to a girls' quilting at Ben D.'s place. They had three quilts in frames, and around thirty girls were there. When Ben came in, he said we sounded like a bunch of *gaxing* (cackling) chickens in a henhouse. I guess we did chatter a lot, but we sang a few songs, too, and got quite a bit of quilting done.

It was such a lovely evening that Rachel and I decided to walk the two miles. On the way over, we passed a lilac bush and each pinned a small bouquet to the front of our capes. On the way home close to midnight, millions of stars were twinkling in the friendly sky. A little breeze rippled through the clover fields, and a screech owl called from the trees.

Pleasant as the night was, I didn't want to walk the rest of the way home alone after we got to Eli's place. Rachel insisted that I stay for the night, as Mamm had felt sure she would do.

In the dark, we tossed our bonnets on the spare bed, chattering all the while, debating about whether we wanted to sleep there or in Rachel's bed. Never once did we imagine that someone might already be in the spare bed. Then we went to Rachel's room.

In the morning we were helping Rachel's mom get breakfast. She said, "Rachel, call Dan and Benny for breakfast."

"Benny? Benny who?" Rachel replied.

"Ach," her Mamm said, "I forgot to tell you that cousin Benny Byler was in the spare room for the night. He came here to catch a van early since he is going with Dan to help tear down an old barn."

At that moment the stair door opened, and Benny and Dan appeared. Each had a bonnet perched jauntily on their heads, with the strings tied under their chins. They danced a little jig around the table. Benny asked, "Who do you think you are, trying to hit me on the head with your bonnets?"

It was so hilarious. He had my bonnet on and was so attentive to me at the breakfast table that I'm sure of it now—he does like me! That's just too bad, for I've done exactly what Mamm told me not to do. I've set my cap for Gideon. I'm quite sure he's going to ask me for a date anytime now. You're just a little bit too late, dear Benny boy, nice though you are.

Lilac time is my favorite time of year, but June with all its beauties is a close second. What Mamm often quotes is surely true: "What is so rare as a day in June?" Those red rambler roses twining up the back porch lattice are out of this world. I've heard that someone said, "If you ever doubt there is a God, look deep into a rose." The fragrance is heavenly and would be recognized even if a rose appeared as nothing but a pot of pitch.

Daed and the boys, and neighbors Eli and Dan are making hay, and that's another scent I wish I could capture and put in a bottle. I pity poor city dwellers who don't know the sweet smell from a field of freshly mown hay.

I must write about the experience we had with bad old Bossy, the cow. I was out in the strawberry patch when it happened and nearly split my sides laughing. It looked so ridiculous and hilarious. Old Bossy was with a new baby calf, way at the back end of the meadow, near the road that goes up to Grandpa Daves. She didn't come up for milking.

So Daed and Peter hitched Dobbin to the *Dachwegli* and drove back there via the road, the closest route. They opened the gate, drove into the meadow, caught the calf, and put it into the *Dachwegli.* They tied the cranky cow to the back of the rig and started to bring them up to the barn.

Bossy trotted along behind nicely for awhile. Then she really got mean and began to yank her tie rope from side to side. That caused the *Dachwegli* to slide back and forth on the road from one ditch to the other.

Poor Dobbin kept trying to look back to see what was wrong. When he spied the cow, he took off at top speed. Then Bossy had a really hard time because she couldn't run as fast as Dobbin. I think she was flying part of the time.

When Dobbin slowed to turn in the lane, Bossy was in command again. Here she had more traction than on the road. She yanked from side to side again. Suddenly the *Dachwegli* just overturned and Peter flew out.

Bossy tore loose and took off. Just at that moment, Sadie opened the chicken house door and stepped out with a basket of eggs. Bossy must have really been feeling mean by then. She ran up to Sadie with her head down, butted her off her feet, and hit the basket of eggs so that it flew up into the air. Smashed eggs were flying all over.

If the calf hadn't begun bawling for its mama just then, it's hard telling what more she would've done to Sadie. The poor girl was unhurt but covered with dripping egg yolks. The men managed to put the calf and Bossy safely into the barn.

As soon as I saw that no one was hurt, I had a laughing fit. At first Sadie was indignant, but after a while, she joined in. The two of us tramped down to the creek and went swimming. But I made sure I stayed upstream from Sadie until she was clean. "All is well that ends well." We had a lot of fun of it.

Gideon has spoken at last, just as I thought he would. I'll give him my answer on Sunday evening, at the singing. I'm as happy and excited as could be. But there's one bad hurdle to jump over yet. I need to tell Mamm and Daed and get their permission for a date.

I know they think I'm too young yet. I know just what they'll say, but I am determined to have my own way this time. I don't think they have a right to dictate about this matter.

In the three months since I started *rumschpringing*, I've gotten to know Gideon a lot better. Though he's dashing and fun loving and not one of the tamer ones, I'm sure it's nothing that he won't outgrow. I think he and I are a lot alike: we just want to enjoy life for awhile.

I'm sure we'll figure out a way to get to know each other better, with or without permission. But maybe I shouldn't have written this. What if Mamm would come across my journal sometime and read it! That would be just too bad.

Ach, it's not one bit fair. I was as cross as could be all day. I finally mustered up the courage to tell my parents about Gideon's question. They acted like I was a child—as young as Sadie! Don't they know how grown-up I am?

They calmly and kindly responded: "We should

have told you sooner, but we've decided we will not allow any of our children to date before the age of seventeen."

Mamm added, "We've heard a few things about Gideon that aren't the best. He may make a change for the better when he's a little older."

"Meanwhile," Daed advised, "make it a matter of prayer."

Hmmph! I *have* prayed about it, and I'm sure Gideon's the one I want and that we are meant for each other. He loves me and I love him. Outwardly, I'll make it appear that I'm obeying my parents. But I'm still seething inside. I didn't say much. I'm not going to let them spoil this for me.

I'll tell Gideon on Sunday night, and together we'll figure out something. We're adults and able to make our own decisions. Besides, it's not really their business whom I date or marry, is it?

August 3
....
Hurrah and hallelujah! We have outwitted them! Yep, we did! It took some thinking and planning, but we accomplished it. We had our date on Saturday night!

Since I've written this much now, I'd better hide this diary carefully. If Mamm or Sadie reads this, I'm in serious trouble. I have a small cedar chest with a key, so I'll lock my diary inside and hide it under blankets and quilts in the big cedar chest. Then I'll hide the key under my mattress.

This is how we set things up. I waited till everyone was in bed and fast asleep. Then I opened the window slowly, carefully crawled out on the back porch roof, crept down to the grape arbor, and slid down the pole. *Ah! Freedom!*

I sneaked out behind the barn and back along the field lane to the road. Gideon was waiting there in his buggy, and off we went.

On the way, I asked, "Gideon, do any of your buddies know what we're doing?"

He shrugged. "A few of them might."

That put a cloud of worry over my head. "Well, might someone tell?"

Gideon assured me, "They'll keep it a secret. They're my buddies, and we're loyal to each other."

Nevertheless, it took most of the fun out of the evening for me.

All we did was drive around and visit. He wanted to take me to the drugstore in town for a soda, but I refused, for fear of someone seeing me. My nervousness spoiled the whole outing for us. I was not able to relax until I had swung myself up that old grapevine pole and sneaked over the roof and safely in the window. But I felt triumphant for outwitting Mamm and Daed. They don't suspect a thing.

August 8
....
Last night we had another date, and this time it was much better—wonderful, in fact. Gideon is so charming. I was on cloud nine and for-

got all my fear and anxiety about being seen by someone who might tell. It's amazing, but since I've gotten to know Gideon a little better, I'm not afraid of anything when I'm with him. He's so sharp and capable of outwitting our "enemies"! He has quite an influence over me. I won't worry about a thing anymore.

As I sneaked in the lane after Gideon had brought me back, I saw two boys running out the cow lane. At first it frightened me badly. But then I realized they were likely Pamela Styer's two teenage nephews who are staying with her for a few weeks this summer. They've been fishing there at the creek every chance they get, and they go jogging past every day to keep in shape for athletics.

Why they would've been jogging after midnight, I don't know. Maybe they had gone to town for pizza and wanted to jog it off.

Oh dear, I was awfully sleepy in church this forenoon. I'm afraid I didn't get anything out of it at all. When I'm older and prim and proper, then I'll make sure I listen to the sermons and keep the *Ordnung* (church rules).

August 11
.... It's Little Crist's job to bed the heifers. This morning he went up to the haymow to put down straw. Suddenly he came flying down those steps so fast it's a wonder he didn't fall and bust his head. Crist was yelling, *"En Shlang, en Shlang!* (a snake)."

I was feeding the calves, and Daed and Peter were milking. Crist's eyes seemed about as big as saucers. He cried, "There's a huge snake up there as big as a telephone pole!"

Daed chortled, and Peter snorted, "Get real!"

"Come, I'll show you," Crist insisted. "I really and truly am not lying!"

Daed led the way up the stairs from the feeding alley, with the boys behind. I gingerly followed, holding my skirts tightly around me. They went up the little ladder to the haymow while I waited anxiously below.

I heard Peter whistle in amazement and Daed say, "*Unvergleichlich* (strange)!"

"What is it?" I shrieked.

There was no answer, so I called, "Is it safe for me to come up and see?"

Still no answer. My curiosity was torturing me anyway, so I started up the ladder. When I reached the top, I found them staring at what looked like the biggest snake I ever saw. I stifled a scream. It indeed was frightening even though it wasn't as big as a telephone pole.

"It's just a snakeskin," Daed said. "But if there's a snakeskin here, there's bound to be a snake somewhere nearby, too."

I glanced around fearfully. "Do you think it came in with the straw when we did the threshing?"

"I don't know," Daed admitted. "I guess we'll have to search the haymow by forking all this straw around. Peter, you go over to Emanuel's to ask the men if they can help, and Crist, you go over to Eli's."

A short time later, a group of neighbor men and boys were assembled with hay forks. I'm sure the story spread like wildfire, and all those who were curious to see such a big snake showed up.

Benny Byler was there, but he never once looked my way. I guess he must have found out how I feel about Gideon.

Sadie and I climbed up on the hay wagon to watch, not wanting to miss the excitement, but afraid to get too close. We expected to hear someone yell, "I found it!" A shivery feeling traveled up and down my spine.

They searched every inch of the big old barn and the area surrounding it but found nary a trace. After awhile they gave up. The boys spread the snakeskin on the driveway and measured it. It was a good ten feet long.

Pamela Styer came over to see what all the fuss was about. When she appeared, I remembered the two boys running out the cow lane on Saturday night. I sidled over to Pamela and asked, "Why haven't your nephews come over to see the snake?"

She chortled. "Wild horses couldn't have kept them away if they were still here. They flew home to Chicago on Friday evening."

So that counts them out. Who else could have been sneaking around here? I wish I could confide in someone about what I saw, but I'd be giving myself away. Perhaps some pranksters have put that snake-skin in our barn just to trick us. I wish I knew.

September 8

My life is too full and exciting just now for much journal writing. The days are getting chilly and the nights cool, and our snake mystery is still unsolved. We are all careful how we step in the barn. Crist makes sure he doesn't wait till dark to put straw down.

I've gotten into the habit of looking back over my shoulder a lot. I half expect to see a monster serpent coming, ready to twine itself around me and squeeze me to death. I've even had a few nightmares, but I'm not going to tell the others how I'm hounded by fears. I don't believe the others suspect that the snakeskin was a prank. I think it was just that, but I'm still jittery.

Now for an update on Gideon. Things are better than ever! In fact, they're getting better all the time. Now don't misunderstand me, dear diary. We never do anything bad. I am not that kind of a person, not at all. We're just out for a good time, and getting to know each other better. There's nothing wrong with that, is there?

October 9

That Gideon! He is something else! I never laughed so hard in my life. Oh, he was so funny. Last Saturday night he told me, "Make sure to be at the farm show in town next Saturday afternoon at one o'clock. Wait for me in front of the town hall. I have a surprise for you."

I told him, "I can't promise. Mamm and Daed will never let me go."

"Then cook up some errand or whatever, and *be there!*"

All week this worried me. I was wondering if I could manage it. Well, luck was with me. Early this morning, Daeds left with Sadie and Crist to visit friends Polly and Allen today. Peter spent the day helping Priscilla and Henry install some linoleum.

I was glad to have the day to myself! I couldn't eat more than a few bites at lunchtime. I was so excited about going. Never in all my sixteen years had I been to the farm show. I got out our trusty old scooter and pushed off for town, all aquiver with expectation. Was Gideon going to take me for a ride on a Ferris wheel or something like that? I couldn't wait to find out.

Standing there in town, I felt awfully conspicuous and out of place in my Amish clothes. I wondered how it would feel to blend right in with the crowd.

After awhile, I heard a ripple of voices and laughter among the people, and then applause and shouting. Coming slowly up the street was a weird sight, a real covered wagon with a lumbering cow hitched to it. Leading the cow was a stooped old lady wearing a long dress and a big straw bonnet.

The crowd was going wild by the time the wagon was directly in front of me. When the weird rig stopped and the "old lady" turned and beckoned to me, I nearly fainted with shock. Finally I recognized

Gideon. He grinned at me and ordered, "Climb in!"

I was blushing with embarrassment and refused at first: "No, no!"

He insisted. "I did this for *you*."

It took all the spunk I had to climb up there and take the reins! The "old lady" took a bucket and a milk stool out of the wagon and proceeded to sit down and milk the old cow. Meanwhile, I had a giggling fit and almost spoiled the whole effect for Gideon. I had to pinch myself to stop.

Halfway through town, we went down a side street, but the crowd's cheer followed us to our destination. Gideon turned us in at the Covered Wagon Restaurant and explained, "I built the wagon for the restaurant. The manager ordered it to display on site as an attraction and an advertising gimmick."

The cow was trucked home, and we spent the rest of the afternoon finding out what a farm show is like. Now, if only no one finds out that we were there. What would Mamm and Daed think?

Tomorrow is our *Faschtdaag* (fast day). When I think of that day being set aside for repentance and prayer, it gives me a sad feeling inside. Oh, I know I am not what I should be at all. But surely it's not wrong to want to have a little fun, is it?

October 22
....
The golden leaves are falling from the maple tree, and my heart feels heavy and sad tonight. I just don't know what's wrong with me.

I'm awfully hard to get along with. I snapped at Sadie today and was rude to Mamm.

Mamm cornered me in the *Sitzshtubb* (sitting room) and asked me, "Aren't you feeling well?"

"I'm all right."

She wasn't satisfied. "You don't seem very happy lately. Can't you tell me what's bothering you?"

I did my best to convince her I was okay, but I never could fool Mamm about my feelings. I came up to bed and had a big cry. The truth is, I have lost my peace and joy. I'm about as grouchy as can be.

I'm defying my parent's wishes, seeing Gideon behind their backs. Sometimes I wonder—is it worth it? But, yes, oh yes, it is, for he loves me and I love him. Even though this sneaking around spoils my happiness for now, it will be worth it in the end, I'm sure.

November 14
··· We're in the midst of the wedding season. I keep thinking that next year I can go to weddings as Gideon's girl. Sadie and I went to see

Grandpa Daves tonight. A full moon was out, and we walked through the field, dodging the corn shocks.

Grandma Annie welcomed us cheerily at the door, then bustled around, bringing us glassfuls of cider and a plate of popcorn balls. We enjoyed relaxing there in their dear, homey, old-fashioned kitchen. Grandpa was telling stories of their expeditions by train or hired van, to see relatives and friends in other Amish settlements. Every now and then, Grandma would add a few words to his story.

The visit nearly brought tears to my eyes. They were so contented, and their home was so peaceful. When they were young, did they ever have conflicts and emotional pain as I do now?

Grandma chided me about losing weight and said that maybe I was gadding about too much since I had started *rumschpringing*. We put a few stitches into the lovely appliqued quilt she had in her frame.

They invited us all to come for dinner on Thanksgiving Day, along with Priscilla and Henry and family; and Barbianne, Rudy, and James. Grandma wants to roast a large stuffed turkey, along with all the trimmings, and the others will each bring desserts.

Before we left, Grandpa went to the cellar and brought up a bag of his prize red Macintosh apples. He sent them along home with us, saying, "An apple a day keeps the doctor away," with the usual twinkle in his eye.

Their friendliness did cheer me up. But trudging home through the cold, frosty moonlit night, my heart felt heavy again. I'm sure that Sadie found me a poor companion.

Those brothers of mine! They took a notion to make some Christmas goodies. Mamm, Daed, and Sadie had gone shopping, so I was boss of the kitchen. I was planning to go to cousin Sara's school Christmas program. So I told them, "You can make whatever you wish, but when I get back, I want the kitchen to be as spotless as I left it. I don't want to see a single dirty dish on the counter or in the sink."

They agreed to that. On the way home, walking through the softly falling snow, I kept wondering how the kitchen would look. Well, when I stepped in the door, I was pleasantly surprised. The kitchen was as tidy and spick-and-span as I had left it, with not a stray dish or kettle in sight. On the counter stood two pans of pecan turtle bars and a batch of Rice Krispies date candy.

I really praised the boys. Though I didn't think of it at the time, the looks they gave each other smacked of some kind of mischief. I didn't give it further thought until they had gone out to do chores and I was preparing supper. In the gas oven I found two dishpans full of sticky kettles, mixing bowls, and spoons! Ei yi yi!

Gideon gave me a lovely watch for Christmas, the kind you pin on your cape. I'm going to pin it under my cape instead, so no one sees it. I don't want Mamm and Daed to find out we're exchanging gifts.

I can't believe that we never got caught while I've been sneaking out on dates. These last couple weeks, Gideon no longer waits for me in his buggy. He comes with friends Fred and Sheila, a young couple from town, in their car. Now we can go places with them where there is no fear that we'll be seen by anyone who knows us.

Whenever I'm with Gideon, it seems as if nothing else matters. Lately I've been comparing us with Fred and Sheila and thinking, *As long as we don't act the way they do, we're all right.* Whenever my conscience bothers me for sneaking out, I quiet it by telling myself, *It'll be okay if we don't do anything bad.*

Our family spent yesterday, Christmas Day, at Priscilla and Henry's house. I got to hold those cute toddlers to my heart's content. They are so sweet!

When we sang Christmas carols in the afternoon, I found myself wishing we'd sing "Jolly Old Saint Nicholas" and "Jingle Bells" and "Up on the Housetop" instead of the hymns. What's wrong with me?

On Sunday night at the singing, Eli's Rachel told me, "On Christmas Eve at midnight, all the animals in the barn bow their knees to the Christ child, because he was born in a stable."

"I don't believe it," I said.

"That's really true."

She had me so nearly convinced that I set my alarm clock for a quarter to midnight, got dressed, and ran out to the barn. I took a gas lantern and was not afraid, since it was Christmas and the starry night seemed filled with peace and contentment. I thought of the carol, "Silent night, holy night! All is calm, all is bright."

In the barn I sat down on a hay bale. I'm not sure if I really expected to see the miracle or if I wanted to prove Rachel wrong. After awhile, I was sure it was past twelve and nothing had happened. I heard noises in the walls (rats?) and started shivering.

Then I happened to think of the snake, so I jumped up and ran for the house as fast as I could. In my haste I forgot to close the barn door. As a result, the waterers all froze by morning and made a lot of extra work for us during chores.

Daed asked, "Who left the barn door open?" The whole story of my foolishness came out. I just hope Gideon won't hear about it. And just wait till I see Rachel again. Grrr!

January 28
··· Swirls of beautiful, nearly pure white snow cover the landscape and make it seem cozy inside at the sewing machine. I kept it humming as I mended clothes while Mamm and Sadie made doughnuts. Mmmm! They sure are delicious.

With all this snow on the ground, I sure don't

worry about the snake anymore. I wish I had thought a little further there in the barn on Christmas Eve. I'd have realized that if there ever was a snake in the barn, it surely would have been in hibernation by then.

Guess what, dear diary! Daed and Mamm are planning a trip to the Midwest before spring, in a few weeks, in fact. Their main reason for going is to visit good friends Isaac and Rosemary Bontrager in Minnesota. I hope they don't have to delay leaving home because of a snowstorm. Gideon and I are looking forward to having a little more freedom for a few weeks.

All winter, my heart seems to be as cold as a stone. I've gone from feeling bad about our deception, to feeling plain indifferent, almost as if I don't care. But I can't and I won't give up Gideon!

Mamm walks around these days looking so maddeningly peaceful and serene. Sometimes I think I could take it better if she'd give me a humdinger of a tongue-lashing. But of course she doesn't know what we're up to, either.

February 12
.... Hurrah! They've gone. Sadie and Crist went along, and Peter and I stayed here to do the chores and keep the home fires burning. Fred and Sheila plan to take Gideon and me to a Valentine's Day party on Monday night. I can hardly wait! I won't wear my Amish clothes, and neither

will Gideon! Sheila said she would loan me one of her dresses, and I'll change in the washroom at a service station.

Now if only I can get my hair in shape. I shampooed it today. When it was dry and I was combing out the tangles, I stood in front of the mirror, thinking vain thoughts. I whirled around, admiring my waist-length crowning glory, thinking, *How soft and glossy and shiny it is! It's such a pity that I have to put it all up in a bun.*

I gave my hair a fling, back over my shoulder. To my horror, I felt a tangled, sticky heap on it. By looking in the mirror—ugh!—I could see a mass of curled, sticky flypaper in my hair! *Ach, Alend* (oh, misery), what a mess! I was horrified and utterly dismayed when I found it impossible to untangle the hair without a scissors!

Oh, my beautiful hair! I had to cut a lot of it out. Just wait till Sadie gets home. She'll catch it from me for putting up that flypaper near the mirror just because she saw a spider run across it. Grrr! *Ya well,* that's one time Mamm was right: pride *does* go before a fall.

February 13
.... A dense fog hung over everything this morning, and my head felt about as foggy as the weather when I groggily got up. It served me right because I stayed up until two o'clock last night reading a novel that Sheila loaned me. It was a pas-

sionate story. I just couldn't put it down until I'd read every page of it.

Only half awake, I trudged out to the feedlot to let the cows in for milking. Then I saw something that made me jerk wide awake, blinking my eyes in disbelief. There, in the side of one of the cows, was an arrow sticking out.

I screamed for Peter, and he came running, looking as frightened as could be. *Was in de Welt* (what in the world)! He couldn't believe his eyes, either. Who would've played such a mean trick on us? The cows weren't even out in the meadow, just in the feedlot. Someone must have been awfully close to the barn last night.

Peter went to the phone shanty to call the vet. Even though it was early Sunday morning, he came right away. He removed the arrow from the suffering cow and doctored her up. The vet thinks she'll be all right since the tip of the arrow didn't puncture any vital organs.

However, it still gives me the shivers and makes me feel jittery. No doubt someone who knew that Peter and I were alone wanted to play a trick on us, to frighten us. What might they do next?

This is our in-between Sunday, when we don't have church in our district. Now we'll have time to recover from all this excitement. Valentine's Day is tomorrow!

I'm still shaking like a leaf and I don't have anyone to talk to. I must write or I shall fly into pieces. I'm all in a panic, trembling something awful. Tonight after bedtime I waited until Peter was asleep, then crept out the window, shinnied down over the grape arbor, and sneaked out to the road. Fred and Sheila and Gideon were waiting there, and off we went to the party, as carefree as could be.

We had a great evening. When they dropped me off a short time ago, I came light-heartedly strolling in the back way. I was quiet, so as not to wake Peter, and thinking that I didn't have to worry about Mamm or Daed waking up and peeking out of their bedroom window.

All of a sudden, I stopped in my tracks. Someone or something was moaning eerily in the bushes. I was absolutely terrified. The sounds then changed to loud groans. The bushes parted, and two white ghosts emerged and came toward me, moaning and groaning all the while.

Too terrified to even scream, I made a dash for the *Kesselhaus* (kettle house). Once inside, I hooked the door and somehow got up the steps and into my room. I dived under the covers in my bed, trembling so bad that my teeth were chattering like crazy. I was nearly scared out of my wits.

After I calmed down a bit, I tiptoed into Peter's room. He was sleeping soundly, so I did not disturb him. Even if I had told him about my scare, how could I have explained why I was outside?

Oh, I wish Mamm or Daed would be here. What if it was a real ghost, out to get me for disobeying? I know I won't sleep a wink the rest of the night. I shall kneel and pray until the sun comes up—if ever it does.

February 15

Last night I fell asleep on my knees, with a blanket draped over me. All day I've been thinking about how short and serious life is. I keep remembering that motto in Grandma Annie's kitchen: "Only one life. 'Twill soon be past. Only what's done for Christ will last."

At our last church meeting, Preacher Emanuel said, "We should not do anything that we would not want to be doing when Jesus comes, and not go any place where we would not want to be found when he returns." How often I would have been found guilty!

Early this morning on the way to the barn, I circled the house and looked around. Back near the grape arbor, by the big yew bushes, I found two old white sheets lying. I am convinced now that it was two of Gideon's buddies lurking there, trying to scare me out of my wits. Probably they are the same ones who put the snakeskin in the barn.

No one else knows about us, so it must've been them. They're probably just jealous. *Ya well*, I can't say I didn't deserve it. I'm wondering and shuddering when I think about facing the judgment day while I'm unprepared. I prayed a lot, too, and I think I am ready to make a decision.

February 20

....

Sunday. The roads were very slick and icy this morning. After doing the chores, Peter and I walked to church, slipping and sliding and picking our steps carefully, to keep from falling. Many families were missing due to the bad roads. By the time we ate dinner, the ice was melted by the bright sunshine.

Peter went home with a friend for the afternoon. Rachel was at her cousin's place for the weekend, so I came home, though I dreaded the thought of being home alone. The main sermon was full of the doom that awaits the wicked. By the time the service was over, I realized that I was utterly wicked.

How could I have been so blind and callous, deliberately disobeying my parents this way! In Old Testament days, persistently disobedient teenagers were stoned to death. I deceived Mamm and Daed and justified my hypocrisy. If only . . .

Evening. Peter has gone to bed, but I know I won't be able to sleep and I won't even try. I just wish Mamm and Dad were here. As I wrote those words "if only," I was interrupted by a knock. When I jumped up and went to the door, there stood Gideon, looking more solemn than I have ever seen him before.

"Did you hear about Sheila?"

Dumbly I shook my head no.

"Her car skidded on the ice this morning and went down over a bank. She's in the hospital, badly injured. Fred asked me to come in and sit with him. Won't you come, too? I've got a driver here."

I could not refuse, though I'd rather not have gone at all. I left a note for Peter, and we were on our way. The drive to the hospital seemed to take forever, but I wished we'd never get there at all.

It was even worse than I had feared. Sheila was lying there in the intensive care unit, her eyes wide open, staring but seeing nothing.

She's in a breathing machine, and her hair is all shaved off her head. I thought, with deep shame, how I had just a few days ago admired my own hair as my crowning glory. What a vain thought that was! How much of a glory is Sheila's hair to her now?

She lies there so utterly helpless, and oh, I know she is not prepared to die. Why, just on Monday night at the Valentine's Day party, she glibly remarked, "I'd rather die than go to church!"

Oh, I have to shudder—it might have been me. I'm sure I'm not any more prepared to die than Sheila. In fact, Sheila would probably be better off than I would be. I don't believe she had the Christian upbringing and teachings and parents that I have.

Now I see my mistakes, how much a rebel I have been, how self-willed and determined to have my own way. I can only say, "O God, be merciful to me, a sinner." What if Sheila never has a chance again to make a change?

This was another bad day. I felt like crying all day, but what would Peter have done then? This morning when I took the basket to gather the eggs, I saw a gruesome scene. The chicken house door was wide open. Something—a fox, raccoon, or dog—had killed most of Mamm's prize leghorn hens. Over thirty of them were dead and lying there, strewn about.

Whatever it was didn't even bother to eat them. It just killed for the fun of it, I guess. Peter thinks it must have been the neighbor's dog. But who left the chicken house door open? Gathering the eggs is my job, and I'm sure I always carefully closed and hooked the door.

Peter teased me a little: "You probably heard the snake rustling in the walls and ran for dear life, leaving the door wide open." Yet I know I left that door securely fastened shut. I suspect it was the same person who shot the arrow into the cow, but there's no way I can prove that. I wish I could.

There was one bright spot in the day. Tonight a carriage drove in, and it was Rudy, Barbianne, and little James. They came to see how Peter and I were making out by ourselves, and they cheered us up.

These days Barbianne is glowing with happiness. James is six years old already, and now they are expecting another little bundle of happiness in their home in June. She asked me to come and help them out, as *Kinsmaad* (nursemaid). I can hardly wait to go.

Mamm, Daed, Sadie, and Crist came home today, and I welcomed them with open arms. I was never so truly glad to see them. I felt like I needed a shoulder to cry on. These past few weeks have been an awful strain.

Twice more we have gone to see Sheila, and there was no change whatsoever. If she lives, they don't expect her to regain all her abilities. She would try to relearn walking and talking, starting over again just like a baby.

I rushed to Mamm for comfort and said, "How glad I am to see you back!" I told her about the poor cow and the hens. But how can I tell her about Sheila without spilling the whole story of me sneaking out with Gideon? I can't even tell her about the ghosts wearing sheets, either.

Mamm was comforting: "The hens can be replaced. I'm just glad you two are all right."

Tonight after the chores were done, we were all sitting in the kitchen, talking and eating popcorn. They had lots of stories to tell about their trip, about Isaac and Rosemary Bontrager and their family in the community there, and about the Amish school they are establishing.

After the other children had gone up to bed, I told Mamm and Daed, "I'm sorry for how rebellious and grouchy I have been the past few months. I want to turn away from all my sins and apply to join church this summer."

They were very happy. Mamm shed a few tears

and said, "I knew this would come. You will find happiness and peace in giving up your self-will."

We talked some more about their trip to Minnesota. Sometime I'd like to go and visit Isaac and Rosemary myself.

It's getting late. My feelings have been stirred up today, and I'm tired. But I think I am on a better track. Good night, dear diary.

March 14
....

It's all over between Gideon and me. My heart is broken into a million pieces. We can't see eye to eye on anything anymore. He just doesn't understand why I won't keep sneaking out to go with him, either.

My heart aches so much to think about it. At the Sunday-night singing, I managed to tell him privately, "I could have been a good influence on you instead of helping to drag you down."

"Down?" he said. "I'm not so bad, am I? I just want to have a good time. So you think you're too good for me, huh? Well, there are other girls that will be glad for the chance to go with me." And he walked off.

I wanted to run after him and tell him how wrong he is and beg him to come back. But something kept me from doing that. I choked back the tears until I was at home in my room.

How often did I write in my journal, "I just want to have a good time"? Oh, how childishly vain I was!

....

I thought I was pretty, I thought I had gorgeous hair. "Vanity of vanities! All is vanity and vexation of spirit." If only I had heeded Mamm and Daed's advice.

I could cry an ocean full of tears, but even that wouldn't do any good.

March 24

Finally I mustered up the courage to tell Mamm everything—yes, everything, even the part about sneaking out by way of the grape arbor. She cried, as I knew she would, and threw her arms around me. She said, "My poor wayward child! How thankful I am that you have confessed!"

I assured her, "I have sincerely repented of being willful and disobedient. From now on, I want to live in obedience and give my heart to God and serve him with all my heart, soul, and mind."

She gave me the *Prayer Book for Earnest Christians*, translated from the old German book that we use in our church services and for family devotions. On the first page it says, "Containing fine prayers, rich in spirit, with which devout Christian hearts may take comfort in every season and in every need."

I know I don't have a very devout heart yet, but I mean to find out what I must do to get one. It's such a heavy load off my mind to have confessed everything to Mamm. Of course, she told Daed, and it is such a blessing to know that they have forgiven me and are praying for me.

Nursemaid and Teacher

April 10

My seventeenth birthday. I'm feeling what Whittier expressed so keenly:

> Of all sad words of tongue and pen,
> The saddest are these: "It might have been."

Here at my open window I sit, breathing in the beauties of a lovely spring evening and thinking back to a year ago when I started this journal. I had such lofty dreams and aspirations then, and I was all excited about entering the thrilling world of *rum-schpringing*.

What a failure I was! A few tears slip down over my cheeks as I ponder Whittier's sad but true words about what might have been. If I had been obedient and submissive, then Gideon and I would be able to start dating now and could have a blessed upright courtship instead of our secret and furtive dating.

Then, too, I think of Benny Byler. He was so admiring and good-natured, and once he had wanted me, too. Now he is going with another girl. Here I mournfully sit, having spoiled everything for myself. How long shall I wallow in regret? Today is Easter Sunday. Christ's resurrection brings believers the promise of new life.

I shall just have to be contented with whatever scraps of usefulness I can gather here and there as I journey life's pathway.

I've heard that happiness is a wayside flower along the highway of usefulness. I wonder what God's will is for me to do.

One thing I know: I wouldn't exchange the peace I have in my heart now for any number of thrills. My goal now shall be to please God in all things. I console myself with precious lines from Evans-Wilson:

> Manlike it is to fall into sin.
> Fiendlike it is to dwell therein.
> Christlike it is for sin to grieve.
> Godlike it is all sin to leave.

May 9

It's lilac blossom time again—the loveliest of all times. I feel as if the pieces of my heart are slowly being put back together again. Healing is taking place. This may be the most blessed summer of my life, while I am taking instructions for baptism and church membership. At times I feel like I am just learning to walk, as a babe in Christ. Sometimes I stumble and slip backward.

Yesterday we had a visiting minister at church, and he gave us an illustration of Christian life. Trying to earn our own salvation or trying to get to heaven without Christ as our Savior is like going into the woods without a compass. We get lost and cannot find our way. We think we are on a straight course but keep finding ourselves back where we started from, defeated and discouraged, and not one whit closer to our goal.

I have to think that if I am ever redeemed and cleansed from all my sins, it will be a great work of grace. Instead of mulling over my failures, I will look to Christ, who is our righteousness, and whose blood washes away all sin.

I have a great bouquet of lavender before me on the chest. Its hauntingly sweet fragrance fills my room with delicate perfume. Ah, springtime, with all its loveliness and sweetness and sadness!

May 19
.... *Himmelferdaag* (Ascension Day). Priscilla and Henry planned a surprise picnic for us and Grandpa's and Rudy's. We had a wonderful day for it, sunny but not too warm. There's a lovely, scenic, level spot down at the curve where the creek has a little island in the middle. In the shade of two tall sycamore trees, we put a picnic table and lawn chairs.

Our four cute little colts were frisking in the meadow with their mothers, a nice picture to watch. Henry had made a fireplace with stones and put a grate on top. He built a fire and roasted hot dogs and

From the Kitchen of:
Priscilla

Chicken Corn Soup:

3-4 lb. stewing chicken
2 T salt   1/4 tsp. pepper
1 1/2 C celery (chopped)
1 onion (chopped)
1 qt. corn   (over) →

hamburgers for us all.

Priscilla brought potato salad and prepared a Dutch oven full of her incomparable chicken corn soup. Barbianne brought *Hans Waschtlin*—mmmm! They're made with scraps of pie dough rolled around an apple filling.

When we were ready for dessert, Mamm sent Crist on his scooter over to the freezer we keep in Pam's garage, to fetch the five-quart pail of ice cream. When he came back with it, we were all ready with our scoops and cones, mouths watering. But when we dug in, behold, it was frozen lard instead of ice cream! What a disappointment!

Grandpa Dave said, "That's so *unvergleichlich* (absolutely) disappointing!"

Mamm sent Peter up to our small refrigerator freezer for a small box of leftover homemade strawberry ice cream for him. When she presented him with a dish of it, he took a spoonful and leaned back in his chair, savoring it in his mouth. With closed eyes and a look of bliss on his face, he declared, "This is the life! How delicious!"

At that moment a bird perched overhead in the tree sent down a glob of you-know-what. It landed ker-splat, right on his glasses. Poor Grandpa! He jumped up, sputtering and coughing. Grandma came to his rescue, using her big white handkerchief to clean off the bird mess.

None of us could keep a straight face. Soon everyone was laughing uproariously. He sure did look comical! What really topped it off was that in the confusion he lost his false teeth. Everyone helped hunt for them, beating the bushes and clumps of grass around the area. No one had seen them fall. We just couldn't figure out what happened to them.

Finally Grandpa happened to reach into the side pocket of his *Latz Hosse* (broadfall pants). There were the teeth, right where he had put them. Sheepishly he put them in place and said, "It's all right for you all to laugh, but it would feel better if it wouldn't be at my expense." In a surprisingly short time, he had recovered his dignity and was telling interesting stories again.

Meanwhile, Sadie and I were listening and also kept busy watching Priscilla's babies. They seemed to have one-track minds, to toddle to the edge of the creek bank and try to dive in headfirst. I think several of Grampa's stories from his great-grandmother's day are worth recording here. They are supposed to be true, though some details might not be accurate since they were passed along by word of mouth.

There was once a poor young widower with three small children, and he needed a wife to help him raise the children and be a mother to them. In his home area, there was no eligible lady for him. He had just enough money left for train fare to a neighboring state where there was a community of his church people. He took his three children with him.

He arrived on a Saturday. First of all, he went to the bishop there and told him to announce something in church the next day. He asked the minister to publish the approaching marriage of him and a certain spinster he knew who lived in the area. He was so sure that she would say yes that he talked to the bishop without consulting her first.

Then he went to the spinster's house, stayed for supper, and made known his intentions. The lady had a mind of her own. She shook her head no and told him firmly and clearly that she would not marry him, and that he must go back home.

The poor widower had no money to go home, so

she gave him enough to pay his train fare. Instead of going home, he took the train for Canada, where he found a kind-hearted woman willing to be his wife. They lived happily ever after, I suppose.

Another story he told was also about a widower. A woman in her late thirties had consented to be his wife. They had been published and were planning to be married on a Sunday at the end of a regular church service.

The wedding day arrived, and eventually the bishop was ready to ask the couple to come forward to be married. However, the deacon's wife whispered something to her husband, and the deacon then informed the bishop that the bride-to-be had slipped out during the service. She had not come back in. There was nothing to do but dismiss the services.

The disappointed widower was very sad. Some days later he decided to talk to the bishop about his troubles. On that same day, at the same time, the woman who had backed out of marrying him decided to talk to the bishop's wife. Neither knew the other was going to the bishop's place.

By now, the single woman was sorry that she hadn't gone through with the marriage. The widower had hiked across the field and was in the bishop's blacksmith shop talking when the door opened. The bishop's wife was bringing the woman to seek the bishop's counsel. Imagine their surprise in meeting each other there, for the first time since the day of their canceled wedding.

The young woman told the man that she was sorry for her actions and now was ready to leave her home of over thirty years. She was willing to carry out her commitment and to cleave to him as her husband. The bishop counseled with them. He decided that since the wedding sermon had already been preached, if they both desired to be husband and wife, he would marry them right there in the blacksmith shop.

So, with the bishop's wife and grown son (called over from the barn) as witnesses, they were immediately united in marriage. Hopefully, they also lived happily ever after.

Peter, Crist, and James had gone for a walk, and came back carrying a crying James. He had stepped into some *Brennesel* (stinging nettle) with his bare feet.

Finally we packed up, and everyone else went back to the house. I stayed out there, lying on a blanket and soaking up the peace and beauty of the afternoon. I was daydreaming and counting my blessings.

Adjoining the meadow was a newly mown hayfield. The fragrant breeze wafting my way reminded me of what Gideon had once said: "Haymaking is my favorite time of year." I wonder what he's doing with himself these days and whether he ever thinks of me. I still can't think of him without a few pangs of regret or shedding a few tears.

I have to think about Sheila a lot. She's in a rehab center now and does not even recognize her own parents. Fred has already forgotten her, apparently. I saw him in town with another girl. Surely the way of transgressors is hard.

June 17
.... Well, here I am at Rudy and Barbianne's place and loving every minute of it! Rudy came for me this morning at eight o'clock with the wonderful news of the arrival of seven-and-a-half-pound Joanna!

She has a head full of dark hair and a tiny upturned nose, the cutest baby I've ever seen. The midwife was still there when we got back. She had kindheartedly agreed to stay until Rudy came with the *Kinsmaad* (nursemaid).

James was brought home from Grandpa Dave's place, and he seemed stunned to see his mother with a new baby in her arms. He kept murmuring, *"Schee glee Boppeli* (beautiful little baby)," and stroking the baby's cheek. He has been an only child for six years. Now he'll have to adjust to sharing the limelight. Barbianne wisely hugged him, too, and told him this was his very own baby sister.

She seemed quite tired and worn, yet radiant with happiness and even exuberant. "Oh, Dora," she cried, "is it really true, or am I only dreaming? I'm half afraid that I'll wake up after awhile and find it was all a dream. Who do you think the baby looks like?"

"Just like you," I told her. "Such a sweet little

bundle. I'm sure you deserve her after waiting all these years."

"I'm sure we *don't* deserve her," Barbianne returned. "God has blessed us so much. All is well, and the baby is healthy and perfectly formed. I thought my cup of happiness was full when James arrived, but now its full and running over."

The midwife had told Barbianne that she must stay in bed and rest for a few days. Hence, I had the delicate job of giving Joanna her first bath. I gathered towels, washcloth, clean baby clothes, and a basin of water on the kitchen counter. Even before I began, little Joanna opened her mouth wide and screamed, waving her little fists and kicking up her heels.

I figured I was off to a bad start. But to my amazement, as soon as I began to actually wash her, the crying stopped and she opened her eyes as if to see what was going on. She seemed to like it. I carefully dabbed each tiny body part with the wet soapy washcloth, then rinsed her and patted her dry. We were finished in a jiffy, and it wasn't bad at all.

Then on with a diaper, T-shirt, and blanket. It was just like playing doll, except that this doll was squirming and alive, soft and warm, cuddly and sweet. My eyes filled with tears to think that such a blessing might never be mine. But I knew I didn't deserve it anyway. So I hugged the little living doll and determined to bravely accept my lot in life, whatever it might be.

Tonight I helped Rudy in the barn, with James tagging along, chattering a mile a minute. He is always on the lookout for Rocky the rooster, who has a bad habit of attacking and pecking little boys. As we were feeding the calves, one of the little critters just wanted to turn his behind toward me and let fly with his hind legs and hoofs.

So we called Rudy, and he firmly showed the calf who was boss. He decided to remove the calf from that box stall. Rudy put a rope on the calf to get him out. The calf was stubborn and refused to budge. While Rudy was pulling with all his might, all of a sudden the calf stepped forward, letting Rudy sit down fast.

By the looks of his clothes, he had a soft landing. James shouted with laughter at the comical sight and looked like he had half a notion to jump into the pile of manure, too. They are a lively, fun-loving set, a happy little family.

If I ever have a husband, I want him to be just like Rudy. I want a little boy like James, and a tiny darling like Joanna. But I've had my chance and ruined it.

Until the day I die, I will rue the bad influence I was on others. I keep thinking that maybe no one will find out besides Gideon's buddies. If that small gang doesn't tell it around, they might save my reputation. Sneaking out at night like that was against my parents' rules but otherwise might appear worse than it actually was. But now I want to avoid even the appearance of evil.

Ya well, it's no use brooding about it. Right now I'm in the middle of a lovely evening. A gentle breeze laden with the scent of Barbianne's rose garden stirs the white curtains at the window. I brought my prayer book along, and one of its prayers expresses my feelings exactly:

> Most beloved Father in heaven! oh, what evil have I brought forth in my short life! Few are the days of my life, and many are my sins. The least of my time I have lived unto you; the most and the best of my time I have wasted in vanity. Oh, how much good have I let slip by, and in comparison, how much evil have I gathered, thereby staining my body and my soul!
>
> Oh, most beloved Father, forgive everything out of grace! Oh, gentle Redeemer, cover up all this with the robe of your innocence and righteousness. Oh, heal my wounded soul with your comfort! Teach me to bear in mind that my life here must end, that my life has a goal, and that I will need to depart.
>
> Behold, my days are the width of a hand and my life is as nothing before you.

June 19

I haven't even gotten *Heemweh* (homesickness) yet, so I must be improving! How could I get *Heemweh* with such a darling little doll to care for? Barbianne needs more rest, so I have Joanna in my care tonight. I'll just take her downstairs for the feedings, and the rest of the time I must do whatever I can to keep her happy and contented. I'll rock her or walk the floor with her if she's fussy.

Now she's sleeping in her little bassinet, her delicately molded features and arched eyebrows sweeter than ever in repose. Was there ever a dearer, sweeter, more perfectly formed baby?

I love my work here, even in the busy time of picking and canning peas and strawberries. We had oodles of peas to put away today. Rudy took them to the pea huller, and that saved us hours of painstaking labor, *blicking* (shelling) them by hand.

James and I picked a bouquet of the loveliest imaginable pink roses, took them in, and put them in a vase at Barbianne's bedside. She says she's so glad that her few days of bed rest are about over now. She pities our grandmothers who had to stay in bed for ten days to two weeks.

Ya well, I'd better get some sleep before Baby awakes. I can't do what comical James tried today. When Joanna was crying, he thought he could just push her chin and upper lips together and she would stop. He loves his little sister dearly, though, and would do anything for her.

June 26
.... We've had quite a bit of excitement here in the neighborhood this past week, more than enough to suit me. On Tuesday, Rudy came home from town with the shocking news that the bank there had just been robbed, and that the robber

was an Amishman! At least he was wearing Amish clothes and a broad-rimmed Amish hat.

The robber escaped on foot. A helicopter was out, circling the sky countless times. It made a loud chopping sound, scaring Rudy's animals. The cows stampeded, and the chickens all crowded into one corner. The horses spooked and acted like they thought it was the wild West, and the dogs howled piteously.

Later Mamm told me that Pam's car came careening in their drive. She was out of breath, saying that the suspect had been seen running north, headed our way. The police with their dogs were out searching. Pam was on her way home. She had forgotten to lock her back door and wanted Daed to go with her and help check her trailer home, to make sure the robber wasn't hiding there.

Mamm went along too. They bravely searched through the closets and basement and every nook and cranny where someone could have hidden. Finally she was satisfied that he wasn't there. Lots of police cars were cruising around by then, with sirens and blinkers going and radios crackling. They ordered everyone to go into their homes and lock the doors.

The suspect had last been seen running north. A white-flag roadblock was set up at several entrance roads, and about a half dozen cops moved into neighbor Eli's barn. With drawn guns, they searched the stables, the haymow, the strawmow, the granary bins, the harness closet, and the outlying sheds. They even looked in the manure pit.

Later we found out that the robber had gone into the bank, waved his gun, and ordered everyone to lie down. Then he emptied all the cash drawers into a bag. He ran to a nearby parking garage where he had a suitcase stashed. After he changed, he carried the Amish clothes in his suitcase and hailed a taxi to go to the next city.

A description of the suspected robber came over the cab radio, and then came orders to call the office. The cabby swung into a Uni-Mart, where the robber escaped, leaving behind the suitcase but not the money.

Neighbor Eli was out mowing hay with his mules, which ignored the commotion. The police ordered him to go into the house at once and lock the doors. They peered into the culverts and searched the young cornfields.

Another helicopter, called in from Maryland, had a special infrared detector that was supposed to be able to locate a mouse in a haystack. However, it couldn't find the suspect. The woods and brush along the creek were searched. Apparently the man had disappeared into thin air.

Eventually the search was called off. Later Eli and the police pieced together what happened.

After the excitement died down and everyone had left, the robber crawled out of his smelly hiding place inside the honey (liquid-manure) wagon, just back of Eli's barn. He sneaked up onto the *Scheierdenn* (threshing floor) and burrowed himself a nest under loose straw in a corner. There he lay in hiding while Eli's were doing their chores.

Eli even went upstairs and threw down straw to bed the steers, not realizing that the robber was in the barn. It's a wonder he didn't stick the crook with his fork. The robber stayed there till after midnight. Then he set out, jogging eastward with his bag of money. Someone reported seeing a jogger.

Almost instantly a half dozen police cars were on the scene. The officers surrounded the suspect, with guns at the ready. They made him lie down, hand-cuffed him, and took him to headquarters. Now he is safely behind bars.

It sure gives me the shivers to think that our peace-loving countryside was invaded this way. I'm afraid that after this I'll need to look behind me whenever I go outside after dark. Since this hap-pened, Barbianne has started locking all the doors and windows, even the cellar and *Kesselhaus* (kettle house) door. Rudy kids her about it, but I don't blame her a bit.

June 29
.... Just a few more days before my job here at Rudy's is over. Sadie wants to come over here for a week or so, too. I've grown quite fond of little James. He follows me around everywhere, ask-ing cute questions. His comical antics amuse me a lot.

Last night at dusk, I was sweeping the *Kesselhaus*. As usual, James was along and wanting to help. He pushed open the back door by the coal bin. I heard him saying, "Ei, kitty, kitty. Ei, kitty, kitty."

I walked over to where he was leaning out the door and reaching for the "kitty." That's when I saw a small black animal with a white stripe down its back and tail—a skunk out looking for grubs!

By reflex, I yelled, "*Bisskatz! Bisskatz* (polecat)!" As its tail shot up, I grabbed James and slammed the door. We ran for the safety of the kitchen. It was a close call. This morning it stank terribly of skunk spray back there at the door.

Baby Joanna grows sweeter and cuddlier every day, if such a thing is possible. I wish I could take her home with me.

July 1
....

I'm back home again. As much as I liked working for Rudy's, it's still good to be home and hearing the warbling purple martins.

In my spare time, I'm studying our eighteen articles of faith, pondering repentance and amendment of life, and reading my *Prayer Book for Earnest Christians*. Rachel and I, along with four boys, are taking instructions for baptism this summer.

On church Sundays, we go upstairs for some teaching by the ministers while the others start singing below. These are meaningful times for me. I wish I could remember all that the ministers say. They call this the most important step we will ever take, giving our hearts and lives to God, and being baptized into the church.

One of them said, "If you humbly come to Jesus by faith, in true repentance and turning from all known sin, God will accept you. By ourselves, we all are poor and sinful. But God will change your lives so that instead of serving your self-will, you will be living for the Lord Jesus Christ, in cooperation with his body, the church."

I can understand, and I want to be changed, but when will God finish changing me? I have the highest of intentions about how good I want to be, how virtuous and righteous, how generous and unselfish, and I ask God to help me. But I can't be with my family long at all, until I've failed again.

This may be a sharp or hasty word, a short answer, an argument, wanting to have my own way, or sparring back and forth with Sadie. I have a habit of bossing Peter and Crist mercilessly. Why can't I be good on and on? Sometimes I feel like giving up.

I talked to Mamm about how discouraging this is to me. She said, "The more inner light we have, and the more 'hunger and thirst after righteousness,' the more we will lament these failures in ourselves. When we fail, we must confess it to the Lord and ask for forgiveness and for help to overcome. One day we will realize that our failures are coming further and further apart."

She gave me this Bible verse: "Blessed are those who hunger and thirst after righteousness, for they shall be filled."

Last Sunday, we had an interesting sermon at

church. The minister told a story about a woman who was a cripple. "There are people whose bodies are crippled, and people whose personalities are crippled. But this woman was crippled physically and emotionally. She was angry, bitter, and depressed about her physical handicap, and she blamed God for her trouble.

"One day a kind minister spoke to her. He told her that God loved her just as she was and wanted her to be his child. He said God had a plan for her life. The minister encouraged her to give herself to God just as she was, with all her bitterness, pride, shame, hate, jealousy, resentment, temper, and fears. If she would give the Lord all those negative feelings, he would take them away and put love in their place.

"The woman did just that, not just once, but over and over again when things happened that were hard to accept. She used her talents to serve the Lord. Many years after she gave her life to God, she wrote a hymn that has helped thousands of people." Then the minister quoted,

Just as I am, without one plea,
But that Thy blood was shed for me,
And that Thou bid'st me come to Thee,
O Lamb of God, I come, I come.

There were more verses. Her hymn has helped me, too. If that woman had all those sins and later became saintly, maybe I can, too.

While I was at Rudy's, it was easier for me to be

good. Now I have a fresh desire to be obedient and helpful to my parents, and kind and loving to Sadie, Peter, and Crist. I have to think of poor Sheila, who doesn't have the chance now to do right. My heart aches almost unbearably. Why, oh why, wasn't I a good example for her?

July 8

Exciting news, dear diary! A letter from Isaac and Rosemary Bontrager of Minnesota has turned my world topsy-turvy! They need a teacher for their one-room Amish school, there in their small community of families. They wondered if I would be willing to come and teach there.

Me? Me, a teacher? Honestly! They offered to let me board with them since it's only a one-mile walk to the school. The teacher they had hired for the coming term has come down with a bad case of Lyme disease. So they're hard pressed to find someone to take her place.

Last year's teacher has agreed to carry on during September and October if necessary. She likely has her wedding planned for the marrying month of

November. So I can have my choice of times. "When would it suit you best to start?" they asked.

I guess it's up to me to make a decision now. Do I want to go or not? Deep down, I want to go: it smacks of adventure, challenge, and excitement. I love children. Priscilla has often told me, "You have a way with children," whatever that means.

School lessons were always easy for me. But could I handle the disciplining part? There are only fifteen pupils, which should be easier than the thirty-five in some of our schools around here.

I was just reading the book *These Happy Golden Years*. Its author, Laura Ingalls Wilder, was a teacher at age fifteen, and small for her age. Some of the pupils were older than she was. I sure wouldn't like that! I'll become eighteen during this school year.

However, that teaching job might not last long. When Becky Yoder recovers from Lyme disease, she may want her job back.

Now there's something else to consider: I just heard this week that Gideon is going to Minnesota to work as *Gnecht* (hired boy) for a cousin of his. Well! I have to wonder, *Does God have our lives all mapped out and planned, or is it just a hit-or-miss thing?*

I'm afraid I'll never be a good-enough Christian to know God's will for me, nor to give up my selfish desires and inclinations if I do know it. Would I really want to step out into the unknown like that? Deep down, I want to be yielded and submissive. But within me are two voices in conflict. How could I leave my dear home and family for up to a year?

Here on the chest I sit as I glance out the window. I see Daed and Mamm out by the barn bank, discussing plans for a rock garden on the side facing the house. Peter is riding his new horse out the cow lane, while Crist awaits his turn. Sadie is in the garden, picking a bouquet of gladiolus and singing to herself. Purple martins glide and swoop around their home, warbling and visiting cheerfully with each other.

How could I leave all these dear familiar scenes of home? Oh, how I would miss them! What if I'd get a terrible case of *Heemweh* (homesickness)? Would they have to send me back? That surely would give me a big piece of humble pie to eat!

Ya well, I've been sitting here thinking for half an hour. I'm no closer to a decision than I was before. I guess I'll take a walk along the creek before I go to bed. Maybe there in the misty meadowlands and twilight, I'll find my answer among flickering fireflies, night insects calling, stars coming out one by one, frogs croaking in the marshes, and a screech owl calling from the trees.

I will trust God to guide me, as Solomon says: "Trust in the Lord with all your heart, and lean not unto your own understanding. In all your ways acknowledge him, and he shall direct your paths."

July 11
....
Today I sent off my letter of acceptance. But now that I've made my decision, I'm still having qualms about it. Mamm tells me, "That's

entirely understandable. I'm sure you can make a go of it."

Dear Mamm! How will I do without her for so long? And Sadie too? In spite of our bickering, we are close. She seems to be naturally kind and unselfish. Meanwhile, I have all the struggles and still can't be good. What will I do without her sweet, calming influence over me?

Sometimes when I think of me being a schoolmarm, I get jittery and have a fit of biting my fingernails. Other times I have a bellyache and feel weak, silly goose that I am!

Plans are that I shall leave for Minnesota as soon as I have been baptized and have taken my first communion. Things should work out well that way, and I hope and pray that I can be a satisfactory teacher.

August 15
.... I wish I could slow down the hands of time, time, so relentless, rushing me on, closer and closer to leaving for Minnesota. At least I feel a bit more schoolteacherish now. I have attended our annual teacher's meeting and had two weeks of summer classes with Aunt Fannie.

Come to think of it, I don't even know what Aunt Fannie's last name is! She's a single lady and has been teaching school for around thirty years. Three of her nieces are beginning teachers, and she agreed to coach them. By special invitation, I was included in the training, too.

I'm suspicious that Mamm had something to do with me being invited. Maybe she was concerned about my youth and inexperience after all and wanted to make sure I had some preparation.

Aunt Fannie lives next door to Allen and Polly, so Polly probably told Mamm about this opportunity. Aunt Fannie is a kind and friendly person, a well-liked and highly experienced teacher. She makes teaching sound like a noble and worthy profession, an interesting and challenging occupation.

I learned a lot there and still have so much to learn and absorb. At first it seemed almost overwhelming, but bit by bit things fell into focus. Now I'm eager to try out my newfound knowledge on a roomful of lovable, bright-eyed children. Aunt Fannie gave us lessons on the best methods of teaching and presentation. She coached us on math and phonics for the lower grades, and then moved on to the higher grades and other subjects.

Aunt Fannie has a battery-operated duplicator. I brought home a whole boxful of duplicated sheets— a real treasure indeed! Now I can hardly wait to see my schoolhouse. I do hope it's little and cute, just right for fifteen pupils rather than a big but half-empty old building that echoes every sound.

I haven't even heard the name of the school yet. I hope it's a scenic, poetic-sounding name. I almost wish I could name it myself.

I stayed with the Keim's for the weekend and really enjoyed it there. Polly is a bustling, motherly sort of person. Her chicks have all flown the nest now except for quiet thirteen-year-old Daniel. He drove me to church on Sunday morning. Try as I might, it was impossible for me to start a conversation with him. We climbed on the buggy, he clicked to the horse, and we were off.

I said, "It's a nice morning, isn't it?"

"Yes."

After a pause I observed, "This is a fine horse you have here."

"Uh huh."

After a longer pause, I asked, "Are you looking forward to when school starts?"

"Not really!"

After another half mile, I tried again. "What are you planning to do this afternoon?"

"Don't know yet."

With that, I gave up and we drove the rest of the way in silence. It's hard to believe that Polly's son could be so shy, as outgoing as she is. I'm sure he wasn't stuck up. I guess he's just going through a stage of bashfulness.

I went home with Loretta (one of Aunt Fannie's schoolteacher nieces) for the afternoon and for supper. Then together we walked to the evening singing, at the same place where the church service was held earlier in the day.

When the boys filed in to sing, lo, Gideon appeared among them. Well, well! He never used to come inside to sing. It wondered me so, could he be turning over a new leaf? What would have brought him over to this district?

At any rate, I hadn't forgotten him as well as I thought I had. The minute I saw him, my heart began to flutter. When he gave me a smile and a wink, I'm sure I blushed as pink as a peach.

After the singing period was over, Gideon's sister Naomi came over and asked, "Do you have a way to get back to Allen's?"

I told her, "I plan to go home with Loretta for the night and then go with her to Aunt Fannie's place tomorrow."

Then she asked, "Would you let Gideon drive you over to Allen's?"

More heart palpitations! I said yes. So Naomi went home with her cousin, and Loretta rode home with them, too.

I got my bonnet and stood waiting at the end of the walk, wondering if Gideon still had the same horse. I was hoping that, in the darkness, I wouldn't climb on the wrong buggy. I needn't have worried. There's no other horse that prances quite like Gideon's does, not even Rowdy.

When Gideon stopped the horse and stepped down for me to climb on, he didn't want to stand. By the time I finally managed to climb on, the horse was rearing. I nearly screamed. It seemed like any second he could fall over backward on top of me. Then down he went, but the next moment was rearing again. Three times he did it, and then refused to go.

Another boy tried to lead him for us, but the horse shook his head angrily and refused to budge. A moment later he lunged forward so hard that it lifted the front wheels off the ground. But we were on our way, surrounded by the whistles and catcalls that follow a new couple—at least the *Yunge* (youths) thought we were new.

I'm so thankful that Gideon's buddies didn't tattle on us. Riding with Gideon seemed almost like old times, yet very different because of changed circumstances and my different attitude. Yes, it was a wonderful ride, so much better than those furtive, stolen dates.

He told me, "My buddies confessed that they put the snakeskin in your barn and also did some other pranks around the barn. There's a man in town who keeps reptiles, and they got the snakeskin from him.

"They didn't say anything about who was under those sheets, acting as ghosts, but I'm sure it was them too. *Ya well*, I hope they pay for their damages sometime. But I guess they weren't counting on a neighbor's dog killing those hens."

I asked, "Is it true that you'll be working as a *Gnecht* (hired man) in Minnesota?"

"Yes, it is!"

All too soon we were at Allen's place. I could have invited Gideon to come in, but I knew Polly wasn't expecting anything like this. Then too, I don't want to really start dating until after I'm baptized. I explained that to him. Though he seemed dubious at first, he took it nicely.

He circled the driveway and stopped to let me off at the end of the walk. With a friendly "Good night!" and a flurry of gravel under the wheels, he was off.

Until next time, I'm sure—although he didn't ask for another date. I suppose once we're both in Minnesota, I must give him another chance. I do believe he's sincere and wants to do what's right.

....
This summer would have to go so very fast! In a way, I'm looking forward to being in Minnesota, especially now that I know Gideon will be there. But in another way, I wish the summer had just begun, and I'd still have several months to prepare.

Sometimes just after I wake up from a deep sleep, the realization hits me anew. I frantically think, *Oh, what have I done, what have I done, consenting to teach school! I'll never make a good teacher. What could I have been thinking!* I reproach myself bitterly for it until a fresh breath of encouragement comes along and buoys me up.

Then I feel confident that I have the makings of a teacher and that it will go well. After all, it's just a small school, only fifteen pupils. In searching my heart, I realize that I've always had a secret longing to teach. Thus my feelings swing like a pendulum, and I waver between dread and anticipation.

Meanwhile, I'll try to enjoy these few remaining carefree summer days and prepare for my baptism. A new batch of sweet corn was ready today. As we all sat at the dinner table at noon, enjoying our roastin' ears, I looked around the table. Seeing everybody happily munching away, I suddenly felt a pang in my heart. For so many months, I won't be able to see the faces of these dear ones at home. I choked up and had to leave the table.

I grabbed a bowl, went out to pick lima beans, and had a pity party by myself out there in the patch. After awhile, the chirping and warbling and gliding of the martins cheered me up. The row of blooming hollyhocks and the marigolds along the fence gladdened my heart, too.

I hope they have flowers and birds in Minnesota. But I know I won't see martins there this fall. They're packing up to head southward any day now and won't be back till spring.

Just now Sadie came into my room and informed me, "We're going boating tonight, the whole family together." So I'll finish this later.

Bedtime. We had our boat ride. It will be a precious memory to take with me to Minnesota. Daed and Peter rowed upstream between the lush, overgrown banks. Then we floated back down in the gentle twilight, with fireflies flickering all around, and soft evening breezes rustling the leaves. The night insects were singing their evening choruses, and the frogs sadly croaked in their rhythmic, throaty, sad way.

Daed told stories of long ago, before any of us were born. Then Mamm started a song. A full moon came up over the trees in the east. I had to swallow a lump in my throat when I thought of being in faraway Minnesota. Would I watch that same moon rising there, and think of these dear ones at home? Would I long for them, pining away with *Heemweh?*

Far off in the hills, a fox barked, and another answered him, likely his mate. With quavering hoot, a screech owl called from a tree. We saw a pair of yellow eyes watching us from the brush along the bank. I shivered, but at the same time I felt safe and secure there on the boat with my family. I wondered, *Why, oh why did I consent to leaving the warmth and shelter of our family to go so far away?*

I think I'll read a prayer out of my *Prayer Book for Earnest Christians*. Those prayers are so inspiring and much easier to understand than in the German. I hope I'll be strengthened and comforted for the task ahead.

August 25
....
Daed is weed-eating tonight, and Mamm's in the garden with her hoe, where she usually can be found in the evening. Sadie is trimming flowerbeds, Peter is washing the *Dachwegli* (carriage), and Crist is stalking around out in the barnyard with his BB gun, watching for sparrows. All these dear, familiar scenes of home—what if . . . ?

Ah, well, I'll try not to mention it again, for I must be brave. If I do get *Heemweh,* I'll make sure that not a single soul finds it out!

Mamm gives me some free time every evening to study the eighteen articles of faith, the Bible, and a few other devotional books she gave me. I'm preparing for my baptism. At the instruction class on Sunday, Preacher Emanuel spoke to us about being church members. "Will you help to build up the church and its *Ordnung* (rules for Christian living), or will you help to tear it down?"

He explained, "If you are faithful and obedient and spiritual minded, you will be upbuilding to the church. But if you are fence-sitters and have a *macht nix aus* (it doesn't matter) attitude, you're helping to tear down the Ordnung. It's something to think about."

Bishop Daniel added, "If you trust in Christ for salvation, accept him as your Ruler as well as your Savior, confess and repent of all known sin, and seek to do God's will in all things—then you are accepted by God and become his children.

"The baptism by itself does not wash away your sins. It is an important sign of God's work of grace in your hearts, since Jesus' shed blood washes away sin. Through baptism, you are received as members in the church."

All in all, it was a meaningful and inspiring session. I wish Gideon would also be in our class and taking instructions for baptism. Does he see the seriousness of life and the importance of taking this all-important step?

September 18
Today I was baptized. It was a sacred and soul-stirring experience, a feeling of

Tut Buße, und lasse sich ein jeglicher taufen auf den Namen Jesu Christi zur Vergebung der Sünden, so werdet ihr empfangen die Gabe des heiligen Geistes. (Apostelgeschichte 2:38)

being lifted to higher ground, to a new beginning. I have been reading *The Imitation of Christ,* by Thomas à Kempis, and think much of it fits my spirit:

I offer unto Thee, O Lord, all my sins and offenses, which I have committed before Thee, from the day wherein I first could sin, to this hour. I offer them upon Thy merciful altar, that Thou mayest consume and burn them all with the fire of Thy love; that Thou mayest wash out all the stains of my sins. Cleanse my conscience from all offenses, and restore to me again Thy grace which I have lost by sin, forgiving me all my offenses, and receiving me mercifully to the kiss of peace.

Sadie and I went for a walk up the old woods road tonight after supper. The crickets were chirping their fall-like tunes, and the night birds were twittering as we crossed the old swinging bridge to the creek pasture. A squirrel scolded us saucily, his bushy tail jerking frantically as he dashed around.

Soon the leaves will turn bright gold, red, and brown; frost will nip the growing things; and I will be in faraway Minnesota, teaching school. My heart felt light and at peace, ready for the coming challenges. I am casting all my cares upon God, for he cares for me.

October 28

I can't believe it's really true, but here I am in Minnesota at last. I arrived at Isaac's place at about four this afternoon. It sure was a blessed relief to crawl out of that van and stretch my legs again. The trip was almost as bad as sitting double-decker in a buggy and finding that a leg has fallen asleep.

I enjoyed the sightseeing, though. I believe I could fill my journal writing about all I saw. We had nice weather to make the trip. It's a bit cooler here than at home. Most of the leaves have already dropped.

Isaac and Rosemary were away on church duties when I arrived. But Rosabeth, Anna Ruth, and a whole string of younger ones were outside to greet me. I started to feel at home right away.

Rosabeth is just a half year younger than I. She's

a charming, friendly girl. I'm sure she and I will be the best of friends. Anna Ruth is just a year younger than Sadie, and they want to be pen pals. Then it's Isaac Jr., Caleb, Mary Anne, Linda, and two-year-old Benuel.

Together we walked to the house, Rosabeth leading the way, and the younger ones staring at me and smiling shyly. I helped to prepare supper in their plain but clean and homey kitchen. When Isaac and Rosemary came home, Rosemary hurried in while Isaac unhitched.

Rosemary greeted me warmly and graciously: "Oh, Dora, how thankful we are that you are willing and able to come and help us out!"

By the looks of things, there is to be another family member in a few months, adding to the eight children they already have.

I mashed the potatoes and filled the water glasses. When Isaac and Matthew came in, they shook hands with me and were as friendly and cordial as could be. My, this is such a pleasant and congenial family, a fine model.

The children had to crowd together on the bench to make room for me. There was never any squirming or pushing or squabbling. This is a home with an atmosphere of peace and goodwill. Yet they're such a lively and interesting bunch, just like I'd want my dream family of five girls and five boys to be.

After supper I helped with the dishes while the others went off to do their various evening chores. Then Rosemary insisted that I shall have the evening to myself, to rest or do as I please, Rosabeth led the way upstairs to our room, apologizing that I won't be able to have a room of my own.

I'll share a bed with her, and there's another small bed in the same room, where seven-year-old Mary Anne sleeps. So I don't expect to have much privacy now. Rosabeth said they're thinking of fixing up a trailer for me in their backyard under the trees, all for my own, where future teachers would live in turn.

So here I am, in our room, scribbling away in my journal. I have my suitcase under the bed, and there's a lock on it, making it a good place to keep my journal. That way I won't have to worry about anyone reading my personal thoughts.

Isaac's have a nice farm here, so quiet and peaceful. The countryside is much more thinly populated than at home. There's hardly any traffic on the gravel side roads. The house looks out over a nice meadow that has a brook flowing through it. With all these trees around, I'm sure there will be plenty of songbirds.

Down in the garden, I can see Matthew and Isaac Jr. plowing the garden with a walking plow. Matthew is manning the plow, and Isaac Jr. is riding and steering the big workhorse. It's hard to believe I'm actually so far from home, for here are trees and gardens and brooks and workhorses and people just like at home.

I wonder what Mamm and Sadie are doing now, and whether Daed and the boys are plowing our garden, too. And Gideon—is he perhaps thinking of me now, as I am of him? He won't be out here until Thanksgiving. Meanwhile, I hope he'll write to me.

While we were doing the dishes, Rosabeth told me that Matthew is writing to a girl in Pennsylvania. I don't think *I'd* like to have a courtship just by mail. It just wouldn't be the same.

Ya well, I've had my rest now, and I should go and see what Rosabeth is doing. Maybe I can be of some help. Five-year-old Linda and two-year-old Benuel just now shyly peeked around the corner in the doorway, and then quickly disappeared, giggling happily. I'm sure I shall like it here. My worries about catching *Heemweh* have melted away.

October 29
.... I spent this Saturday at my schoolhouse, with retiring teacher, Irene Swartzentruber. She helped me get acquainted with the books and the curriculum. How well I got my wish: the schoolhouse is little and cute, nestled in a hollow with trees around it and a wild rose hedge along the back. I'm so glad it's not big and bare with high ceilings, and a haunted, spooky feeling to it.

It's called Birch Hollow School, a nice and fitting name. It got its name from being in a hollow surrounded by trees, birch trees among them. Behind the schoolhouse are two outhouses, one with a hat carved in the door, and the other with a bonnet.

Inside the schoolroom are old-fashioned desks

Birch Hollow School

with fold-up seats. Everything smells of being fresh-ly cleaned and scrubbed with pine oil. Irene told me that the school mothers got together on Friday after school and gave it a thorough cleaning, all in readi-ness for the new teacher.

The room looks real cozy and inviting. It will soon be even more so, with children's art on the walls and the bulletin board decorated. Irene even had the scholars take down their former art, in readi-ness for what I assign them to make.

Irene is really nice and thoughtful. I think it's too bad that she can't keep on teaching this whole term. However, it's becoming common knowledge that she will soon be published to be married, probably around the end of November. I hope I'll be invited to the wedding and that Gideon will be here by then.

I'm getting to be quite eager and excited about my first day of teaching, which will be on Monday. Another part of me is trembling in my shoes and wanting to flee. But I've put my hand to the plow, and there's no turning back now.

I keep going over all I learned at the annual teacher's meeting, all the gems of wisdom and bits of advice and speeches by teachers from Amish com-munities all over the continent. I feel it was a blessed privilege to be there. If I can remember and follow all the wisdom I gleaned there, my teaching career should be a success.

Also, I want to remember what Isaac told me tonight: "Don't depend on your own strength. Without help from Above, nothing good can come from our efforts. Seek the Lord's help, guidance, and wisdom, for his strength is made perfect in our weakness."

His words humbled me. Maybe I've been planning too much to go forward with my own effort. *Ya well*, if I have, I'm sure I'll be cured of that in a short time, once I actually start teaching. I'll probably have to eat plenty of humble pie yet!

Ho hum, this is Saturday evening. I see that this family is just like ours at home in one way. They're still busy with last-minute chores in getting ready for *Sunndaag* (Sunday). Matthew is washing his buggy, and Rosemary and her daughters are *rischding* (preparing) desserts for tomorrow dinner.

The younger ones are playing, throwing a ball over the shop roof, and calling "Andy-over, piggy-tail." It all seems so dear and familiar, just like at home. I'm thankful beyond words that they accept me almost as one of the family. I seem to fit in so well with such precious, lovable friends.

October 30
.... I just came home with Matthew from attending the young people's singing. I'm too full of various feelings to sleep, so I'll scribble my thoughts in my journal before I go to bed. I lit the kerosene lamp, making as little noise as possible. I'm thankful that Rosabeth and Mary Anne are still peacefully sleeping.

Rosabeth thought it was almost too hard to bear

that she wasn't able to go to the singing. But she woke up this morning feeling sick and feverish, so it was out of the question. I just hope I won't catch something from sleeping with her. Wouldn't that be something, sick for my first day of teaching!

I felt somewhat lost, going to the singing without her, and meeting all those *fremmi* (strange) girls alone. But Matthew put me at ease. Driving with him was quite enjoyable. He is so gentlemanly, and we talked a lot. He wondered about the young people in my home community. We were comparing our ways and customs.

Matthew was hoping I'd know his girl, Ida, but she lives twelve miles away, in another district. I told him about Gideon. He was quite interested and is looking forward to his arrival here in November. "The more the merrier," he said. "Our group is small compared to yours at home."

I made out all right at the singing, too. The girls all seemed to be glad to see me, a newcomer, and warmly welcomed me. I felt at home right away.

Ach mei, I'd better hike to bed right away and get my beauty sleep. It's after midnight, and I don't want to be tired and sleepy my first day of teaching. If only I'll be able to sleep now.

October 31
.... My first day of teaching is now history. I have to admit that I had more than one episode of weak, trembling knees. But all in all, things

went according to plans, actually real well at times, to my surprise.

In the morning my stomach felt fluttery as I started off on the one-mile walk to school. I feared I was coming down with Rosabeth's flu. The closer I got to my school, the more my spunk seemed to dwindle. But then a cardinal began to whistle from the tall pine outside the schoolyard, a rare thing for October, and my heart felt cheered.

I noticed the beautiful hills all around, and thought of a verse: "I will lift my eyes unto the hills. From whence comes my help? My help comes from the Lord." A calm courage seemed to fill my heart.

Isn't it something how, in the hard places of our lives, we automatically turn to the Lord for help? But when feeling self-confident and capable, we don't feel the need for prayer and forget about it.

Maybe too much of the time I'm a fair-weather Christian. Often I feel unworthy to partake of the riches of Christ, too self-centered and carnal minded. I wish I'd know how to keep the right spirit within and be worthy of having God's love and peace in my heart.

There's so much I don't understand. I wonder how I can teach dear, tenderhearted youngsters who each have a soul that will live with God for all eternity. There is so much for them and for their teacher to learn about life besides the three *R*'s (readin', ritin', an' 'rithmetic.)

The children called out a cheerful "Good morning" to me as they came into the schoolhouse to put away their lunchboxes. That gave me a good feeling.

When they ran out to play until bell time, I almost wished I could join them.

I walked around the room, admiring the various pencil boxes, toy pencil sharpeners, and other items on the desks. Meanwhile, I was eyeing the clock nervously. Finally the big hand pointed to six. At last it was 8:30! My hands trembled as I pulled the bell rope and listened for its peals over the playground.

Then, merrily and expectantly, they came trooping in the door and found their seats. Irene had made name cards for each pupil and taped them on the front of each desk. That was a big help to me. Even so, I'm sure it will take several days for me to remember each child's name.

At first, my knees shook at the sight of those fifteen eager faces before me and the realization that I am their teacher, just "poor me." I wanted to greet them all with a formal "Good morning," but I was afraid my voice wouldn't work. Finally I got it out: "Good morning, boys and girls."

It worked! In unison they all said, "Good morning, dear Teacher!"

After that, I had more confidence as I read a chapter out of the Bible to them. Then we bowed our heads in prayer, reciting the Lord's Prayer together. That prayer somehow gave us a feeling of unity and strength.

The rest of the morning seemed to go extremely well. I'm afraid I began to secretly exult in my ability to be a teacher. I thought of the lines of a poem I once heard:

I'm queen of a beautiful kingdom.
God gave it to me for my own.
My subjects are dear little children,
My desk in the classroom my throne.

Just at that moment, what did I see but the quick thrust of a hand, and a paper airplane sailing across the room. A pair of mischievous yet scared and guilty brown eyes met mine. My heart seemed to sink to the tips of my toes. That was Elmer, and already he was trying me out.

I tried to put on a firm front to cover my quaking spirit: "Bring that airplane to my desk. And then I want to see you at recess time."

What, oh what, it wonders me, would I have done, if he'd have refused to obey? The rest of the pupils were respectful and obedient all day. I suppose I should be thankful and try to overlook that small misdemeanor.

Not till the middle of the afternoon did I realize that we had forgotten to sing in the morning. Red-faced and blushing, I told the class to file to the front of the room. They did so, with questioning looks on their faces until I passed out the songbooks. Then there were snickers and smirks on a few faces. I felt my courage dwindle to nothing, for the umpteenth time.

Ach well, I survived the day, and now I'll have to hie myself off to bed before I collapse in utter exhaustion. I'm so bone weary tonight. Somehow, somewhere, I'll have to get the courage and ambition to go back again tomorrow. Help, Lord!

.... My life as a schoolteacher
seems to be falling into a routine, at least to a certain
extent. I've gotten acquainted with all my pupils and
matched the proper names to the faces. I've found
out that, from tall Willie in the eighth grade to sweet
little Eunice and Mary Anne in the first grade, they
all are different and lovable, each in their own way.

The four from Isaac's family are Anna Ruth in the
seventh grade, Isaac Jr. in the fifth, Caleb in third,
and Mary Anne in first. Isaac Jr. is alone in his grade,
leaving him without any friendly competition. But
he's so smart that maybe with a little extra coaching,
we can promote him to the sixth grade with Johnnie,
Elam, and Mary.

Willie is alone in eighth grade, but we can't promote him higher, and it wouldn't do to put him back
in the seventh. He says he doesn't mind being the
only one in his class. In the second grade are pretty
Rebecca, with graceful airs, and Joel, whose elfin face
and twinkling eyes remind me so much of my brother Crist.

Cute Caleb and active Andy are in the third
grade. In the fourth are Laura, with the angelic face
and wistful eyes, and mischievous Elmer and Noah.

I think the most challenging but sweetest to teach
are the first-graders. Mary Anne and Eunice like to
come up to my desk and talk whenever they get the
chance, and I'm glad they do.

Yes, I'm actually beginning to feel like a real
schoolmarm, bustling around, giving assignments,

checking papers, and answering raised hands.

It's exciting! But, *ach*, I'm so glad it's Friday night. Now I can lay aside my schoolteacher's "mantle" for a few days and be a carefree girl again. I'm tired and I think I've lost weight this last week or so. Even my cape doesn't fit as snugly as it used to. Sigh.

November 6

I'm back from the singing with Rosabeth and Matthew. The youth group is small here, but they are all friendly and jolly, and it can get quite lively at times. Just three more weeks, and then Gideon will be here. I can hardly wait! No matter how stimulating, the singings will always have something vital missing without him. This afternoon I wrote Gideon a friendly letter and hope to receive one back soon.

I enjoy the drives with Matthew and Rosabeth. The farms are far apart here, and the drive tonight was ten miles. That's at least an hour on the road each way. So after two hours of visiting with Matthew, I feel I know him as well as Rosabeth. I'm beginning to think that Ida of Pennsylvania is quite blessed. I must say, I admire Matthew quite a lot. There's nothing shallow about him.

Matthew will make Ida a good husband. I wonder how soon the wedding will be and whether I'll be invited, or even if I could go if I'd be invited. A trip back home would appeal to me already. I guess I miss my family more than I have cared to admit.

This morning I also rode to church with Matthew and Rosabeth. Isaac gave the sermon on the text. I was impressed with what he said and will write a few things down lest I forget them. He talked about treating others right and trusting in God.

Isaac said, "To love means to love that which is unlovable, or it is no virtue at all. To forgive means to forgive that which is unforgivable, or it is no virtue at all. To hope means to keep on hoping against hope, when things seem hopeless, or it is no virtue at all."

He also spoke on the verse "Be ye therefore perfect as your Father in heaven is perfect." He asked, "Why would Jesus tell us to do something that is impossible?" Isaac explained it this way: "I believe Jesus meant for us to have perfect love and perfect trust in him and to strive for perfection in these things."

Isaac's message makes sense to me. *Ya well*, I'd better crawl into bed with Rosabeth, lest she thinks I am off my rocker for sitting up and writing when I should be in bed. We usually talk for awhile before sleeping, whispering so as not to awaken Mary Anne.

November 13
.... *Birch Hollow School. Birch Hollow Schoolmarm.* I love the name of my school. I love teaching. I love my pupils. My little first-grade girls are the sweetest and most enthusiastic students.

Mary Anne and Eunice haven't mastered the English language well yet, which can be amusing at times.

One recess the lower-graders were playing tag, and Eunice fell and somehow ripped her dress. She came to me with tears coursing down over her cheeks and said, "My dress is *verrisse* (torn)."

The other day I asked her to make a sentence using the word "Dick." She thought awhile, then said, "The paper is not *dick* (thick)."

Trying not to laugh is the hard part. Sometimes as soon as the last pupil has left the room, I sit and laugh at these things. Today when I asked Mary Anne to describe what the girl in the picture was doing, she said, "Caring the kitchen," meaning sweeping the kitchen. For the next picture, she said, "*Drickling* (drying) the dishes."

Both the first-graders have their two front teeth missing, and that makes them so cute. I wish I'd have at least one little boy in that class, too.

November 16

The day started out happily enough. Last night we had our first real snow that amounted to anything. As I walked to school, I gazed in awe at the snow-covered fields, the drooping pine boughs laden with snow, and a bright red cardinal flitting from branch to branch.

It was a clear frosty morning. The cold air stung my cheeks and numbed my fingers. When I stepped into the schoolhouse, a fire was merrily crackling in the stove, and it was already nice and warm. Willie had come early and opened the draft on the stove. He sat at his desk reading a library book, and we chatted a little. He casually mentioned that his cousin is going to come and work for them around Thanksgiving time.

My ears perked up at that and I wondered, *Could it be that Gideon and Willie are cousins?*

I asked, "Is your cousin's name Gideon?"

"Yes," he said. "Gideon was planning to come, but now his younger brother plans to come instead."

What a blow! I kept thinking all day that maybe it was not so, but my heart was heavy. When I came home, a letter was waiting for me on the clock shelf, from Gideon. It was short and to the point. It's true. He's not coming to Minnesota after all. A good opportunity arose for a job with a carpenter crew, and he jumped for that instead. His uncle, Willie's dad, thinks he can make do with his younger sixteen-year-old brother, Sam, in his furniture shop.

Gideon didn't say a word about us writing to each other, only that "We'll see each other in the spring when you return. I'm not ready to go steady. Maybe it would be better for me to date around for awhile, and you can do the same."

I could hardly eat even a bite of supper. When Rosabeth offered to help correct workbooks, I gladly accepted and soon crept off to bed. My head was aching fiercely. I guess I had been counting on Gideon coming more than I realized. I fervently wished I had never come to Minnesota at all. Hot tears stung my cheeks as I thought of my family at home. Here I was stuck in this faraway place.

For awhile, I cried. Then I began to realize how babyish I was acting and scolded myself. I began to pray and soon felt better. I believed when I accepted this job that it was God's will, and I still believe that. I want to submit to whatever path in life the Lord has for me.

If Gideon finds himself another girl while I am here, I'll accept it as God's will and dedicate my life to being a good teacher.

December 5

....   With Isaac's family, I attended the wedding of Irene Swartzentruber and Dan Hershberger last week. I couldn't help but think about how I had looked forward to Gideon being around to accompany me at the wedding activities. Now it's all over.

I keep thinking of the song, "My ways, my child, are not your way. My thoughts are higher than yours." I will give my all to the task of teaching.

Just now I'm making plans for a Christmas program of some sort. We'll sing lots of carols and maybe put on a short skit. Each pupil will have a poem to recite. The parents will provide a covered-dish dinner at the school. Then the students will exchange presents, each giving one to the person whose name they will draw two weeks in advance.

I'm getting enthused about it all and just hope

everything will go well. We had some unwelcome excitement at noon recess today. Second-grader Joel wanted to lick some ice off the water pump, and his moist tongue froze fast to the ice. I was sitting at my desk checking papers when I heard him screaming. It struck panic to my heart, and I rushed to the door.

The poor boy could not get his tongue loose. Some of the other little ones were crying and carrying on, too. Trying to think fast, my mind seemed to go blank.

Eunice asked, "Should I go and get the ax to scrape his tongue loose?"

"Yes—no, I don't know—wait," I replied in desperation.

Then Elam jumped into action. "Teacher, I'll get the teakettle. Hot water will get it loose."

Willie beat him to the door and came out carrying our bucket of cool drinking water. "Don't use the teakettle," he cautioned. "It would burn his tongue."

We poured the cool water over the poor tongue. Sure enough, that loosened it. His tongue, lips, and one side of his cheek had frostbite, and his face began to swell. I wrapped him in a blanket. He cried for water but couldn't drink it until we got him a straw.

I sent Willie with a request for Joel's dad to come and take him home. Poor little Joel!

Meanwhile, the children and I decided to record each day's temperature on the calendar. We also put up a chart of warnings and notes about coping with winter freezes.

I guess it's good I have these distractions, and I

am busy getting ready for the Christmas program. Yesterday I received a letter from Sadie, and she wrote that Gideon had a date with Benny Byler's younger sister Anna last Sunday night.

Mamm wrote, too. Although she didn't write anything about Gideon, I'm sure Sadie told her. I could tell that she knew how that news would make me feel, for her letter was so sympathetic.

Using words from a hymn, she comforted and encouraged me: "God moves in a mysterious way, his wonders to perform. Often the clouds you so much dread are filled with mercy and shall break in blessings on your head."

December 27

Another Christmas day past. Matthew, Rosabeth, and I went caroling with the *Yunge* (youths) here, on a big bobsled pulled by two workhorses. As the group went from place to place, the special bells on the harnesses jingled merrily. We sang for the old folks and the shut-ins in the neighborhood and community. Then we came back home for doughnuts and hot chocolate.

I enjoyed it so much! My happiness does not depend on whether or not Gideon is here, praise be! I am getting over him. But I do not care to go through such an adjustment again!

A few days before Christmas, a big box of presents from home arrived in the mail, mostly homemade gifts and goodies. I was as delighted as a child.

Now for the biggest news of all! Baby David arrived at this house yesterday morning, weighing eight pounds and nine ounces, a fine and healthy baby. The younger ones were quite excited about it, and the older ones too, though they didn't show it as much.

My, this house is bursting at the seams. I wonder when they'll get my trailer home ready. Rosabeth is sleeping downstairs on the *Sitzschtubb* (sitting-room) couch to care for baby David at night.

They put Benuel's crib up here in our room, and I have the care of him at night. That isn't much, just offering an occasional drink of water and seeing to it that he stays covered. He has become attached to me. Today he followed me around, calling me "Dolly," much to Matthew's amusement! It's not that he knows what he's saying. He's just trying to say "Dora."

I don't believe there's anyone cuter than Benuel with his big blue eyes, blond curls, and his lisp. I wish he were mine, so I could take him with me when I leave here.

We had record-breaking cold today. At the supper table, Isaac remarked, "We ought to write it on the chimney."

Rosabeth wondered, "Where does that expression 'write it on the chimney' come from?"

"Ask the teacher, the smartest one here," responded Matthew.

I was silly enough to blush. But happily, I did remember Grandpa Dave talking about it, so I knew what to say. "That custom started years ago when they didn't have enough paper to record special happenings. Grandpa Dave said that when he was a boy, their 1812 farmhouse chimney had things written in German on the white plaster."

My reputation was saved once again. I hope Matthew was impressed. Silly me! I can't imagine what life would be like with no paper to write on. No wonder Grandpa Dave saves every stray envelope and paper that comes in the mail. That's how he was taught, out of necessity.

Ya well, I must get some sleep.

January 1

New Year's Day! My, the time has flown since I came to Isaac's. Over two months already! I like it here, and I like being a schoolmarm, that is, if Elmer behaves. I can't understand what's going on. Some days he's as good as gold, and then at times he would try the patience of a saint.

His work is done so *schusslich* (hurriedly), and he almost always has to do it over. Won't he ever learn to do neat work?

One day he brought to school a small tin can of baked beans. At the first recess, Elmer put it on top of the stove so it would be warm for his noon lunch, but forgot to open it first. The can overheated and exploded, and beans flew all over! What a mess! The floor, walls, and front desks were smeared with beans, and we had a major cleaning job on hand.

However, I was able to use the experience as an object lesson on the power of steam. We talked about how steam engines work, and I assigned Elmer to copy a sketch of the inner workings of one from the children's encyclopedia.

As if that wasn't enough, in the afternoon Elmer poked Laura with his ruler, and then snapped a wad of paper across the room with his suspender. In exasperation, I took a piece of chalk, drew a circle on the blackboard, and told him to stand there with his nose in the circle until I tell him to sit down.

To my embarrassment, while he was meekly standing there, the door opened and visitors arrived. They were none other than Perry Hershbergers, Elmer's parents. I'm sure I'll never use that form of punishment again! At least Elmer was a model of good behavior the rest of the afternoon.

Enough of school troubles! I guess I'll go down and hold baby David awhile yet. He's so sweet. I long to see Baby Joanna once again, too. According to the letters I receive from home, she's growing fast and can already sit by herself. I can hardly believe that she'll be nearly a year old before I see her again.

January 21

Tomorrow is our in-between Sunday, with no church services. The ice is thick enough now, so Felty Yoders had a skating party for the *Yunge* (youths) tonight on their farm pond. I had a wonderful time. The weather was clear, and the sky was studded with millions of twinkling stars.

We were gliding and whirling over the clear and smooth-as-glass ice as we played tag. I couldn't help but notice what a superb skater Matthew is. I thought, *It's a pity that Ida can't be here.*

After the game was over, Matthew came swooping over to me and turned on the spot amidst a shower of ice spray. He extended a gloved hand, and off we went. It seemed like I was flying through the air, yet secure, almost like having wings. I had an exhilarating feeling, with no fear of falling at all.

However, all good things come to an end. A moment later he was gone, disappearing into the darkness, and I rejoined the group of laughing, chattering girls.

The boys then started a bonfire on the bank. Someone brought down a canteen of hot chocolate and doggies to roast. Gideon's younger brother Sam was there, and he is as different from Gideon as night is from day. Gideon almost flaunts his good looks, but Sam is on the quiet side, not a bit wild. Good for him!

February 14
.... The countryside is covered with swirls of beautiful, fresh snow, a dazzling sight. At school we exchanged homemade valentines. I had to think back to the days when Gideon gave me homemade valentines bearing flattering verses. I felt a twinge of sadness somewhere deep in my heart.

The memory of my rebellious time saddened me most of all.

Once I heard a preacher say that when God forgives our sins, he blots them out and remembers them no more. I wish my sins could be blotted out of *my* memory, too. But maybe remembering serves a good purpose, keeping me humble.

We had a pleasant surprise this afternoon. There was a knock on the door, and Willie's parents brought an eight-quart hand-cranked freezer full of homemade blueberry ice cream and *Hans Waschtlin,* scraps of pie dough baked with an apple filling.

Will Sr. is a great storyteller. He went up front and entertained us all with a few good tales. One was Lewis Miller's story of Bolly Weddle.

This boy had many adventures in trying to support his brothers and sisters while his mother was in the hospital. They lived in their covered wagon by a quarry. His father had been killed by wolves in the forest, so the burden of caring for the family fell on Bolly.

That's one book I haven't seen yet, but I mean to read it. I love books like that. They're so interesting and wholesome. I wish I'd have the whole set at school for all the pupils to read. It was an enjoyable afternoon.

March 7
....

I believe I have cabin fever. I m tired of seeing slushy snow, mud tracked onto my freshly washed classroom floor, and rows of dirty boots and steaming mittens by the stove. I'm longing to hear a robin joyously singing, a turtledove's plaintive cooing, and the friendly little song sparrow's tune.

Yesterday morning little Eunice came up to my desk and said, "Teacher, my head scratches."

"Do you mean it itches?"

"Yes, yes, that's what I mean, and it's bad!"

I thought, *Oh dear, not lice!*

Then Mary Anne hurried up, too. "My head itches, too," she complained.

I glanced around the room. Several of the boys were also scratching their heads. My heart sank. I asked, "How many of you have itchy heads? Raise your hand if you do."

Most of the hands went up. *Ach, Elend!* (misery). A check of the heads verified my fears. The dreaded critters were there. So I dismissed school early and sent a note along to each family:

> Everyone must be treated for lice before they may return to school.
> *Danki!*
> Dora, the schoolteacher

Then I rushed home to Isaac's. Rosabeth and I worked our fingers to the bone, so to speak, washing heads, washing bedding, pillowcases, caps, and scarves. Matthew teased us about getting so rattled and excited about a few tiny insects. But I just hope all the other families do the same. If any don't do it properly, all our work could be for naught.

I'm bone weary and hope that in my sleep, I won't see lice crawling. Why did God create lice, anyhow? Maybe I can assign my older students to find out if lice do anything that is useful.

March 26

I'm back from the singing with Matthew. It was a pleasant drive, with soft, spring-like breezes. Rosabeth went to a friend's home for the night, I could have gone, too, but I decided to come home and get my beauty sleep. Besides, I don't often have the chance to drive alone with Matthew.

Maybe I should be ashamed of myself for writing this, but I could be jealous toward Ida of Pennsylvania. Matthew will make her a fine husband. Nevertheless, I'll claim him as an older brother until he gets married.

Yes, I might as well admit it, old journal, that I think highly of Matthew and enjoy being with him. It feels so right and comfortable and at ease. I wish he'd be free and unattached, but he's not, and I will obey the Golden Rule in this matter.

Besides, I'm sure that if he would know how wild I once was, he'd never consider me anyway. Will my whole life be more doses of regret?

Of all sad words of tongue and pen,
The saddest are these: "It might have been."

Lilacs and Love

In only nine days I'll be eighteen—no fooling! This will be my first birthday without my own dear family around me to celebrate. How time marches on!

I can hardly believe that the school year is already so near its end! I was invited to a *flick-un-schtrick* (mend-and-knit) party at Will Bontrager's today, with all the school mothers. They planned it for this Saturday before an in-between Sunday (no church tomorrow), so I could attend.

The women brought hand sewing, mending, knitting, or what have you. Their tongues flew about as fast as their needles. The potluck dinner offered quite a variety. It was so interesting to hear about the ups and downs of their daily lives, a real tonic to me. I got to know my pupil's moms a lot better. I'm glad to know that they accept me and appreciate me and are able to overlook my faults.

Matthew drove me over and then came back to fetch me home. Rosemary couldn't be there because baby David had a cold. It was kindhearted of Matthew to run around like that for me. What makes him so wondrously—what could I say?—he's just different from how he used to be. . . . Maybe he's planning to get married soon and practicing his courtesies.

When I hopped off the buggy, I said, "Thanks, Brother!"

He looked at me with an expression of surprise on his face. But he rallied quickly and responded, "You're welcome, Sister."

An amusing incident happened tonight. A *Schtedtler* (town) lady came for eggs. When she saw baby David, she exclaimed, "Oh, what a pretty baby! What did you name her?"

Rosemary smiled in amusement. "His name is David. All Amish baby boys wear dresses until they're much older."

The lady was quite embarrassed and could hardly get over apologizing. She needn't have minded it so. Maybe we can chalk that up as an April fool joke that worked.

April 5

Today our settlement received word of destructive tornadoes in Kansas. There is much damage, and they're calling for volunteers to help clean up. Several MDS (Mennonite Disaster Service) busloads from Ohio will be going. Also, a bunch of young men and boys in this area will be leaving for Kansas in a few days.

Matthew put in his name to go along. We'll miss him. If I wouldn't be teaching school, I'd apply to go along, too. A few women are needed to help cook for the hard-working men.

I can't imagine what it would be like to go through such a storm. How frightening it must be to see a funnel-shaped cloud heading your way and realizing that it's not just a bad dream. How tough to see firsthand the agony and suffering, the shock, unforgettable horror, and extreme destruction.

I had a letter from Priscilla and Miriam Joy. Thinking about them all, I had a short attack of *Heemweh* and sad and lonely thoughts. I hope that in Pennsylvania, they will be safe from tornadoes. Then I heard the pitter-patter of little footsteps in the hall. There came Benuel with his stack of little books, saying, "Dolly, Dolly, read me a story. *Buch guck* (look at a book)."

He loves it when I tell him stories out of his treasured little Golden Books. By the time he ran off to play again, my heart was greatly cheered. How I'd love to have a little boy just like him someday.

April 6

Every day Willie drives to school with his pony and spring wagon and brings Mary, Johnnie, Noah, and Laura along. One day last week, a car with a man and a lady drove in front of them. The man got out, went to the pony's head, and took hold of the bridle. The smiling lady came over to the children, offered them a bag of candy, and then held up her camera and snapped a picture.

The next morning they stopped again with more candy and even asked if the children wanted to go for a ride in the car, which the children declined. Every day since then, the strangers have stopped and talked. I've sent a note home to the parents to make sure they are aware of this. What if they are child molesters or kidnappers?

Soon all these school worries and cares of teaching will be a thing of the past. I'll be back home with Mamm and Daed, sleeping in my own bed again, listening to the purple martins warbling and chirping, and feeling myself as free as a bird.

Tonight I'm feeling a bit blue and homesick again. Maybe a walk out in the fresh air will cheer me up. The blackbirds are calling. The earth is moist and black, smelling of manure and growing things. And the lilac bush in Isaac's yard is budding. I hope they don't freeze yet before blooming time.

April 7
.... Matthew is planning to leave for Kansas in a few hours. I have a lot to write about, dear diary.

The monthly board meeting, the last one for this term, was tonight. The board members and their wives were all there, plus most of the other moms and dads. Becky Yoder is the girl who had been planning to teach here at Birch Hollow but caught Lyme disease. She still isn't well enough to promise to teach next term.

So they put the question to me: "Are you willing to teach again next term?"

"Yes," I told them, "I will. But if in the meantime Becky recovers completely and wants the job by next fall, I'll let her have it."

Then they started discussion about a place for the future teachers and the possibility of moving in a house trailer. Mahlon Swartzentrubers had another idea. "The *Daadi* (grandparent) end at our house is empty. Maybe the teacher could live there." Their farm is just one mile south of the school, the same distance as Isaacs are north of the school. All the parents agreed to this proposal and were glad the problem was solved so easily.

Next, the board voted for a new treasurer and tax collector, and each family paid their remaining share of the expenses for the current year. They laid plans for the end-of-year school picnic, what day it suited to have it, and what each family will bring. Everyone helped to sing a parting hymn. After a brief prayer, the meeting was dismissed.

Isaac and Rosemary stayed until everyone else had gone, as we usually do, so I could lock the door. Just as I was turning off the gas lantern, the door opened and Matthew came in. He spoke a few words to his parents, and Isaac and Rosemary left. To me, he said, "I'll walk you home if you don't mind. I'd like to talk with you."

"Delighted," I told him, secretly wondering, *What now? Is he going to ask me to go along to Kansas to cook for MDS?*

Outside, millions of stars were twinkling softly in the sky, and a gentle fragrant breeze stirred the birch leaves to whispering. I was thinking, *Walking with Matthew seems so good and so right. But what would Ida think?*

We made some small talk as we strolled along. When we were nearly home, Matthew said, "I guess you didn't know that Ida and I haven't been writing to each other for quite awhile now. I asked Rosabeth not to tell you."

I shook my head dumbly, not remembering just then that Matthew wouldn't be able to see such a movement in the darkness.

He went on: "I've been wanting to ask you a question for quite awhile now, but decided to wait till the end of the school term."

Why was my heart acting queerly by then?

"I'm wondering if you would care for my friendship? You needn't answer me now. I'm leaving for Kansas at three in the morning. So you'll have some time to think it over before I get back."

For a long moment, I was struck speechless. When I managed to find my voice, it was only to stutter and fumble. "Y—yes, uh, I mean—yes, I'll think it over."

Then he went to the barn to check on a cow, and I came up to my room in a daze, to pour out my feelings into my journal. I am excited and filled with awe and amazement. In a way, I'd want to run out to the barn to Matthew now, and tell him, "Yes, oh yes!" But of course that would not be proper.

I will pray about it and seek God's will. My thoughts are running in circles. I feel shame about how headstrong I was when Gideon first asked me out. I am wondering what Matthew would think if he knew how wild I used to be. I rejoice now and want to do God's will. I know I won't be able to sleep a wink.

May 2

The last day of the school year is over now, and I am waiting for my first chance to go home, but definitely not before Matthew gets back! I remember thinking that when my school term would be over, I'd be a bird out of a cage. Instead, I'm just feeling almost lost, rather aimless, now that the challenge of teaching my lovable, eager-faced pupils is over.

We had our school picnic in the meadow at Willie's place. The families that had too far to walk came in market wagons or spring wagons, bringing big roast pans of scalloped potatoes, chicken potpie, and baked corn. Others brought salads or desserts. In the afternoon several hand-cranked freezers of homemade ice cream were uncovered from insulating bundles on the wagons.

I had a big surprise when Mrs. Mahlon Swartzentruber presented me with a big package. Inside was a lovely friendship quilt made with sixteen embroidered patches. On fifteen patches were the names of the pupils, one name on each patch. The

sixteenth patch had "Birch Hollow School" on it.

Overcome with surprise and gratitude, I barely managed to stammer my thanks. Now if I'd have been their faithful teacher for five years or so—but a gift of a quilt after not even a full term of teaching— it was too much! I'll cherish that quilt for years to come.

One by one the parents came and expressed their appreciation and gratitude to me for coming out to Minnesota to teach their youngsters. I don't feel worthy of the kind words and compliments I received. I guess I'll store their comments in my treasure chest of memories for the next time I feel blue about my weaknesses of the past.

Right now my heart is singing. I'm counting the days till Matthew will be back. I received a birthday greeting from him in the mail, so I think he must have an inkling of what my answer will be.

May 7
....
Lilac blossom time! Tonight I had my first real date with Matthew! As we were driving to the singing, I told him that my favorite time of year is when lilacs bloom. Soon we were passing an old-fashioned wild lilac bush loaded with fragrant blossoms. Matthew called "whoa" to Captain, his handsome new chestnut horse with four white legs and a white star on his forehead.

He jumped out of the carriage, broke off armfuls of the heavenly scented blossoms, and twined them onto the horse's bridle and harness until he looked like a flower garden. Then he picked a particularly choice blossom for me to pin on my cape. We were riding in style! Of course, we removed the blossoms before we arrived at the singing so the others wouldn't make fun of us.

It was such a lovely evening. The sky had a faint pink tinge as the sun set behind the clouds in a maze of glory. This was an evening I'll never forget, extra special because it was our first date *and* our last one until I come back next fall to teach. We talked about my leaving and how far apart we will be all summer.

Matthew teased, *"De weiter de Wege, de schenner die Maedlin* (the further the miles, the prettier the gals),"* quoting an old Dutch saying.

Ya well, I guess writing letters will be second best. I thought back to how disappointed I was when Gideon didn't come to Minnesota. Now I rejoice that he didn't show up. Matthew will be much better for me, and Mamm was right, as usual. If only I had not disobeyed my parents. If only Matthew doesn't find out about my escapades.

May 25
.... Dear diary, here I am at home and in my room. This is my usual place, on the chest by the window. I'm listening to the martins warbling and chirping around their house, and the clatter of the push mower as Sadie and Crist mow the lawn.

Peter just opened the gate for the cows after

evening milking, and they're contentedly heading out the cow lane to the meadow. Daed's out in the field, and Mamm's in the garden with her hoe. Back to the dear scenes of home, the peace and contentment, the familiar, comfortable atmosphere.

Oh dear, I started to cry. Only now do I realize how I have missed them all! I don't know whether I'll have the courage to ever leave again, even for Matthew. I feel like I could crawl into bed and sleep for a week—sweet, blissful, and carefree slumber.

June 28

My, the weeks are flying by on work-laden wings! The sweet summer days will be over before I'm ready. My weekly letters from Matthew are a fountain of life for me, the highlight of my week.

I used to think I wouldn't want a courtship by mail, but it's not half bad, not when you know it's only for a summer. My letter writing to Matthew partly takes the place of writing in my journal. I guess that's why I laid it aside for so many weeks. Then too, I'm kept busy helping Priscilla four or five days a week.

Since I came home, she has taken newborn twin babies whose mother is in prison. They are fair-skinned ones this time, a boy named Brandon and a girl named Brittany. The babes are so sweet, and I feel so sorry for that mother. How sad it must be for her not to be able to care for them and love them!

Priscilla and I have had many a heart-to-heart talk in these past weeks. In some ways, I think she understands me better than does Mamm, my adoptive mother. Priscilla is my birth mother, and she too went through a time of self-willed rebellion when she was young. She knows all about the sadness and heartbreak it brings later on.

Miriam Joy looks up to me as a big sister. That makes me want to do all I can to be a good example for her in everything I do. If she follows in my footsteps, I don't want her to be led astray.

Ya well, I'd better quit my scribbling since we're going for a boat ride tonight. I wish Matthew were here and we could go boating all by ourselves.

July 19
.... I've enjoyed going to the singings here in the home community this summer. One night I saw Anna Byler climbing into Gideon's buggy, and then they were driving off together. But it didn't give me even a pang. I have heard that he's done some growing up since we parted and is making a real man out of himself.

Benny Byler will probably be getting married in November already, if rumors are correct. He's two years older than I. Neither of these could hold a candle to Matthew. I am happy, happy, dear journal, that Matthew is my beau, and not one of them. The day that I will see him again is coming closer and closer.

August 28

Where has the summer flown to so fast, like a swift-winging bird or a flash of lightning? Today we did have a hard thunderstorm, lots of lightning and heavy rains. The creek is muddy and roaring, overflowing its banks. It is an awesome sight, wild, and rushing on and on, until it reaches the mighty Susquehanna.

Tomorrow I leave for Minnesota, back to being the schoolmarm of Birch Hollow School and back to Matthew. I'm all excited about going. I've got butterflies in my tummy, as Miriam Joy would say.

Last evening, before the rain, we had an old-fashioned family gathering, a farewell party for me. Grandpa Daves, Henrys, and Rudys were all here, and we ate pizza and homemade ice cream.

Thinking of leaving all these dear ones brought tears to my eyes. Little Joanna was toddling around on unsteady feet. When I picked her up and hugged her, I was reminded of little Benuel and how he loved me and called me Dolly. I felt pulled in two directions, a part of me wanting to stay here and a part of me longing to go. Will life always be like that?

September 2

Here I sit in my cozy little kitchen in the *Daadi* (grandparent) end of Mahlon Swartzentruber's farmhouse, even though I'm not a grandma—not yet! At times I feel like pinching myself to see if this is for real or if I'm only dreaming.

In my living quarters there's a cute little Gem-Pak wood-and-coal stove, all ready to start a cozy fire in, once winter winds start howling. An old-fashioned grandmother's clock ticks loudly on the wall shelf, and there's a blooming geranium on each windowsill. An old-fashioned hickory rocker is sitting in the corner. The table is covered with shiny new blue-and-white checked oilcloth.

There's a tiny *Sitzschtubb* (sitting room) next to the kitchen, and an equally tiny bedroom. It would be neat to have my scholars' friendship quilt on my bed here. But it's safe at home in my hope chest, awaiting the time when I have a house of my own and a spare bed to keep the quilt on. For now, there's a cheery trip-around-the-world quilt on my bed that Willie's mom loaned me, to stay here also for future teachers.

All the furnishings in this *Daadihaus* were loaned, except the stove, which belongs to Mahlons. A door in my *Sitzschtubb* goes over to Mahlon's *Sitzschtubb*. It's nice to know that they're right there. I think now that I wouldn't have liked it well to live all alone in a trailer.

When I arrived here yesterday, after a stop in the Amish community of Holmes County, Ohio, my home was all ready for me! Last evening the Bontrager family came to visit and welcome me back, all except Matthew. He'll be here tomorrow to take me to the Sunday evening singing. I was disappointed not to see him yet, until Rosabeth told me he's two counties away, helping to dismantle an old barn. He won't be back until today around suppertime.

When the Bontragers walked in the door last night, the first thing I noticed was how much baby David has grown. Then a mischievous little face peered around Mamm's skirts. In a flash, little Benuel was in my arms, crying "Dolly, Dolly." Only then did I realize how much I had missed them all. They are such a dear, precious family.

Rosabeth stayed for the night. We talked and talked, until way past midnight, catching up on a whole summer of news. Now that we're almost sisters, we'll have even more in common. We both think a lot of Matthew, and we see eye-to-eye on many other things as well. I'm glad, for I shouldn't like to have a sister-in-law who isn't a kindred spirit.

Ho hum, I'm yawning, and it's high time for some beauty sleep. I spent all day at my school, preparing, and Monday will be the first day with the students.

September 3

.... Seeing Matthew's big white-sox chestnut horse coming up the road gave me heart palpitations. But once I was on the buggy seat beside him, it seemed just like old times except that he was a little more dear and handsome, and a little more tanned than I had remembered him.

The first thing he said to me, after "hello," was "It's too bad there are no blooming lilacs to be picked now, isn't it?"

"I pressed a sprig of those lilacs you picked for me last spring," I told him. "I've saved it in a book."

"I hope that means you won't forget me," he responded.

Then we were talking happily away, as if making up for lost time. We had a beautiful evening, even without fresh lilacs. It was a joy to be at the singing with old-time friends again.

While driving home, a large, nearly full moon was casting its enchanting glow over the valley. Once at home, we walked down to Birch Hollow School and sat on the porch steps, reminiscing of days gone by. We even talked a bit about the future. Too soon the movement of the moon showed us that it was time to go.

Back at the *Daadihaus*, I sat at the window and watched his buggy lights receding in the darkness. He had only two miles to go. I wondered if he would be willing to drive fifteen or twenty miles for me, if necessary, with his horse. As the old saying goes, *"Was die Liebe treibt is ken Wege zu weit* (what love propels is in no way too far)."

September 4
.... Rain was falling in torrents this morning as I got ready for my first day of school. This is quite a surprise after last night's full moon in a clear sky. Mahlon's wife, Lydia, came over with a big umbrella and a word of encouragement.

I had just started off when along came a horse pulling a market wagon. It was Perry Hershberger, bringing Elmer, Rebecca, and Eunice to school. With a hearty "Whoa!" Perry stopped his horse. Elmer quickly scooted to the back seat with Rebecca and Eunice, and Perry told me to hop on. Perry was quite jolly and friendly, so I guess he forgave me for making Elmer stand with his nose in a circle on the blackboard. Ha!

At school, I rang the bell and stood there in front of my seventeen eager pupils with their friendly faces and smiling "Good mornings." Circles of warmth chased each other around my heart. I felt that the rewards of teaching were well worth the effort.

The three new little first-graders shyly returned my smile. Then with a pang I remembered that Willie had graduated and was not there this year. I would miss his helpful ways.

I have four of Matthew's brothers and sisters as my pupils. I will have to be careful not to make teacher's pets out of them or to give them special treatment or favors.

Ya well, I'm so tired tonight that I can't think straight anymore. My sentences are rambling around. Maybe I can write more tomorrow.

September 5
Last night I was exhausted but happy, with a satisfying feeling of tiredness. Tonight I am not only exhausted, but blue and discouraged as well. I can't believe what happened on my second day of school, after my good year last year. Oh dear, what will the rest of the term be like?

This forenoon at first recess, Mary Anne asked me to come out and see the twig house they had built under the trees. In passing the woodshed, I thought I heard muffled voices and laughter. I paused, straining to hear, and sure enough, I hadn't just imagined it! I peeked into the window, and there was Elmer, looking at a book, with upper-grade boys crowding around to see it.

The next moment a pair of startled eyes was raised to mine, and instantly there was a scrambling to get the book out of sight. To the woodshed door I marched, inwardly trembling but putting up a bold front. In the sternest voice I could muster, I demanded, "Give me the book you were looking at!"

No one made a move, and my heart sank way down. I tried with all my might to keep my voice from shaking. "What did you do with the book, Elmer?"

He motioned to the coal bin. "I put it behind a loose board."

Yes, he had spoken the truth. There behind the board I could see it, but I was unable to get it out. I sent Isaac Jr. for a claw hammer and sent the other boys to their seats. With Isaac's help, we pried loose a few boards and pulled out the book.

With a sigh of relief, I saw that it was only a comic book. But now, what shall I do with the boys and Elmer? He was the one who brought the book, knowing full well that comic books are not allowed at school. As we left the woodshed, I quickly thought about suitable corrective action.

Back in the classroom, I gave the upper-grade boys a lecture: "Now, boys, some comic books are just funny—that's all. But if we make a habit of looking at comic books, it fills our minds with silly, empty stuff, not good, worthwhile thoughts. Next, we might want to look at books that aren't fit for anyone to read.

"The Bible tells us what to think about. I am going to write Philippians 4:8 on the blackboard. You are all to copy it neatly into your composition book and memorize it so you can recite it here in school on Friday morning."

They groaned, but I did not relent. I knew the parents would back me up if necessary. I added, "Elmer, you broke the rule and brought that comic book to school. I am giving you an extra assignment. I want you to pick out a good book in the library, let me approve it, and then read it and write a report on it to share with the school before the end of September."

I just hope this is making an impression on them. I want to be firm with the pupils right from the start to make sure they cooperate in the months ahead. "Totally exhausted" surely describes me tonight. I must get to bed before I collapse.

October 7

What lovely fall weather we're having! According to the almanac, the wooly worms, and the acorns, we'll be having a mild winter, too. Hickory nuts and acorns are scarce. The goldenrod is bright yellow, and the frost is on the pumpkin.

Today is Saturday, giving me some free time. I went for a walk across the corn stubble fields. Then I followed the very brook that flows through Isaac's meadow, came by a beaver dam, and wished I could see them at work. I could use that scene to challenge my pupils. *Ach, well*, at least I have Solomon's proverb about the hard-working ant.

School is going well. The parents have been taking turns to invite me for supper. Last Tuesday we received a message: "Bring no lunches tomorrow." Promptly at eleven o'clock on Wednesday, Joe Millers came driving into the schoolyard with their big hay wagon. The scholars and I jumped on the back, and Millers took us to their home for a hot meal.

They had a long table set up in their big kitchen. We had a scrumptious meal of potato filling, baked lima beans, macaroni-and-cheese, broccoli salad, and plenty of desserts. It was quite a treat after a steady diet of packed lunches at noon.

Joe's children brought in a cute little dog named Lucky and sat him in a box on a stepstool. They tossed him tidbits of goodies, which he caught in midair and never missed once. After dinner we sang a few songs while Lucky curled up in the box and took a nap.

Driving back to school in the back of the hay wagon, I felt as happy as could be again, being the Birch Hollow schoolmarm. The case of the comic book at school seemed like a minor annoyance.

My Sunday evening dates are the highlight of the week. In two weeks we'll even have a Wednesday evening date, if I get to work with Matthew. We're invited to a cornhusking party at Junior Millers. I'm already looking forward to it. What if Matthew finds a red ear? Will he actually give me a kiss?

Keeping house here in my little *Daadi* quarters seems almost like playing house. Even the cleaning is fun, done in almost no time at all. After all, I don't have children tracking in dirt, and there are few dishes to wash.

It's great, having my own place instead of boarding with another family. Isaac's family is nice, but with their growing brood, they don't have room to spare. Anyhow, since Matthew and I are dating, it's likely better for us to be living in different places. That way our times together are more special.

Yesterday we had Hobo Day. The scholars came to school wearing old patched, oversized, and ill-fitting clothes. Some even had their lunches wrapped in burlap, tied to a stick, and carried over the shoulder.

This afternoon we divided into two teams and played Lemonade. Team A chose something to act out, then came marching out to the middle of the room, calling, "Here we come."

Team B: "Where from?"

Team A: "New Orleans."

Team B: "What's your trade?"

Team A: "Lemonade."

Team B: "Get to work, you lazy bums!"

They each took an imaginary egg basket on one arm, bent over, and pretended to be gathering eggs from under the hens, every now and then saying "ouch!" from being pecked by a hen.

Team B made several wrong guesses. Then Elam

guessed right and whispered his idea to the others. All together they shouted, "Gathering eggs!" and dashed forward, trying to tag as many of team A as possible as they ran for the safety of the other wall.

They looked so comical with their hobo clothes on! In the midst of the uproar, a knock sounded at the door. There stood Laura's parents, arriving to visit school. I hope they don't get the idea that we're so boisterous every day!

We had our cornhusking bee at Junior Millers, and I got one of my wishes. I did get to husk with Matthew. It was so much fun, working together in the crisp fresh air, under starry skies. Another bright full moon overhead lent its charm to the countryside. The wind sighed through the willows and spruces in the fencerow. No, Matthew didn't find a red ear! Poor me!

Matthew has taken to imitating Benuel and calling me Dolly. He hardly ever calls me just plain Dora anymore. Sometimes he even says, "Adorable Dora!" That's almost as good as a kiss!

December 19

I've been sadly neglecting this old journal of late. The weeks just fly as if on wings! The Christmas season is here. I love to sing the dear old Christmas carol hymns again.

At school, we're in the midst of practicing for a real program, with several plays and skits, reciting poems, and singing carols. Elam seems to be a born actor, so I'm having him as a leading character in several plays. Matthew will be there to see the program. I'm hoping all will go well and that the pupils all remember their parts.

The *Yunge* (youths) were invited to a taffy-pulling party at Perrys on Saturday evening a week ago. What a sticky, stringy, unruly mess we had! The stuff has to be cooked just right or it won't pull nicely. When Perry saw our predicament, he decided to help. Soon he had taffy in his hair, taffy in his beard, even some on the floor, and of course some in his mouth.

All the *Yunge* were laughing so hard they could hardly pull anymore, and the taffy kept getting stickier and stickier. It just wouldn't harden. Poor Mrs. Perry looked so crestfallen, but I think Perry just liked the attention. Maybe somebody should put a good recipe for taffy in *Die Botschaft* so we all know how to do it right. At any rate, it gave us an evening of fun!

January 5
.... Tonight we had school board meeting, and I rode the one mile to school with Mahlon and Lydia. It was bitterly cold, so I bundled up in layer upon layer of clothes. The snow lay all around, deep and crisp and packed hard on the road. Millions of stars twinkled overhead in the clear, cold sky.

I think we were all surprised to see Becky Yoder

there. She said, "I'm almost completely recovered now of Lyme disease. I'd be willing to take over the teaching at Birch Hollow School starting February the first, if Dora agrees to that."

Well! At first I was inwardly indignant, thinking, *The nerve of her! This is my school! I am the Birch Hollow schoolmarm.* But after a bit I simmered down and gained mastery of my spirit. I remembered that, in consenting to come for another term, I had offered to hand the school back for her to teach if she recovered enough by fall to do that.

It took her a little longer to recover, but I see her point. After all, she was hired for this school before I was, and it's only fair of me to give her the chance. The board members said, "It's entirely up to you. You're not obligated to give up your job."

In the end, however, that is just what I did. *But oh, oh, whatever will I do now?* I thought.

After the meeting was over, I bundled up again. Matthew came for me with Captain hitched to the sleigh, and we went for a fast, exhilarating ride through the glittering, icy countryside, back to the *Daadihaus.*

On the way, I told Matthew, "Becky is ready to have her job back. I guess if nothing else turns up, I'll have to head for home around February first. Becky will want to move in at Mahlon's *Daadihaus.*

Matthew assured me, "Something will turn up if you're willing to work as a *Maad* (hired girl). They're in demand. There are never enough *Maade* to go around."

One thing is sure, dear diary: I don't want to go back home just now, and Matthew doesn't want me to go either.

January 15

Matthew was right. Something did turn up. Enos Millers need a helper, and they want me as soon as possible. Today I received a letter from Enos's wife, Betty. She hasn't been well all winter, and now the doctor wants her to go to the hospital for surgery to remove her spleen.

The Millers have nine children, with the oldest just ten years old and the youngest just one. So that will be a heavy responsibility for me to step into! If I didn't want to stay here so badly, I think I'd steer clear of it and head for home.

It spites me to leave my cozy little home here in the *Daadihaus*. Tonight the wind is howling around the corners and piling snow into deep drifts. It wonders me whether we can have school tomorrow.

February 1

Early this morning I arrived here at Enos Millers. Enos came for me with the sleigh. It was a cold and frosty five-mile drive, into another district for church and school. Enos isn't much of a talker, so I was glad when we reached his home. I rushed inside to warm my nearly frozen toes and fingers near the stove.

As I thawed out, I looked around. In every direction I saw work staring me in the face. *Mei, ach, mei!* I just stood and stared back in dismay for a few minutes. *Elend! (misery). What have I gotten myself into,* I thought.

The kitchen cabinets were cluttered with dirty dishes, crumbs were under the table, and the remains of breakfast were still on the table. A girl of about six years old lay sleeping on the settee, with a pail by her side. *Oh no! Not stomach flu!*

A voice from the bedroom was calling me. I quickly took off my bonnet and layers of wraps, hung them on a hook behind the stove, and went into the bedroom. Betty lay there in bed, obviously not feeling well, but she gave me a welcoming smile.

"I'm so glad you're here. Everything's a mess around here. There are loads and loads of laundry waiting. That's the first thing to be done.

"Dannie, Enos Jr., Uria, and Neil all had the stomach flu, but they're back in school today. Now Laura is down with it yet. I'm just hoping the rest of the family doesn't take their turn, too.

"The water in the furnace kettle is boiling. You can gather all the dirty laundry and sort it in the washhouse. Oh dear, I feel sorry for you having to do our dirty work like this." She lay back on her pillow and closed her eyes, and I noticed that the tired lines on her brow did not relax.

"Don't worry about me," I told her. "I'm just glad to be of help." I meant every word of it. But by the end of the day, my spirits were drooping. When I'd dipped the pails of boiling water out of the furnace kettle and filled the wringer washing machine, I ran into a problem. I yanked and yanked on the starter cord until I was too tired to go on, but it wouldn't run.

I went to the barn to hunt for Enos, but he was nowhere to be found. Back to the washhouse I trudged to yank some more. Soon I was tired and frustrated and mad at Enos for not being there to start the engine. Just then I saw him driving in the lane, bringing the four preschoolers home from the neighbors. *Why didn't he tell me where he was going?*

He removed the spark plug, squirted a little gas in the hole, replaced the plug, and then started the engine. By the time I had those piles and piles of laundry done, it was past time to start dinner.

Five-year-old Atlee set the table for me, but four-year-old Leona and three-year-old Marie complained of bellyaches. Side by side they sat on the rocker, looking about as sick as Laura was.

I fixed a bottle for baby Katie and took her upstairs to her crib. When I came down, Leona was crying and whining, "*Mamm, ich bin grank* (I'm sick)." I made room for her on the settee, at the end away from Laura, and found a pail for her, too.

Quickly I scanned the gas refrigerator for something to reheat for dinner. Any minute now, Enos would be coming in. The refrigerator was nearly empty—not even a stray leftover. I guess I'll soon learn what it takes to keep a large family like this fed, when they're feeling well.

I found a flashlight and headed to the cellar for

potatoes, canned meat, and vegetables. Dinner was far from ready when Enos came in. He helped with the children while he patiently waited and didn't even complain when the potatoes were flat and tasteless. I had forgotten to add salt!

This afternoon, bringing in the half-frozen wash was more of a job than hanging it out had been. I had to drape it around to finish drying in the kitchen, filling all the dryer racks and all the available hooks on the wall. Oh dear, I wonder if I'll ever get caught up with all the work here. Will all this half-frozen laundry be dry by the time washday arrives again?

I'm afraid it will just be work, work, work from dawn to dusk. What an awful grind! Am I really sure I ever want to get married? Poor Betty!

Tonight I went upstairs to my cold room, lit the kerosene lamp, and crawled into my cold bed so I wouldn't freeze while I poured out my feelings into my journal. Every bone in my body aches with fatigue, and my spirits are at an all-time low. Why did I ever consent to coming here? Oh, oh, I'm afraid I'm beginning to feel a little sick. What if I'm starting with the stomach flu, too? *Ach, Elend!* (misery). I just hope there's a chamber pot under the bed.

February 14

Betty has been in the hospital for a week now, and this is the day of her surgery. Enos is plenty worried about her. At mealtimes and when he's in the house, he's like a great silent bear except for grunting a few words of directions to the children. When he isn't inside, the little children scrap a lot and can be downright pesky. They miss their mother, the poor things.

I have so many responsibilities, so many things to remember. Who would have thought that mornings could be so hectic? There is breakfast to make, many lunches to pack, and first-grader Laura's hair to comb and make into a bun. I'm so glad the four oldest are boys. I don't know how I'd manage to get more girls' hair done. With a sigh of relief, I send the last one out the door. But then the day's work has just begun.

February 17

Last evening Enos hired a van driver to take all the children and me to the hospital to see their mother. Poor Betty! How hard it must be for her to not be able to take care of her family. The children crowded around her bed. It was touching to see how glad mother and children were to see each other again, especially little Katie. When we had to leave, she cried as though her heart were broken and then sobbed herself to sleep on the way home.

Most of the other little ones fell asleep, too, and had to be roused when we got back late that night. It was quite a hassle to get them all carried or led into the house, stuffed into pajamas, and tucked into their beds. Enos had to check on a cow in the barn, so I didn't have him to help.

In the darkness and commotion, I never noticed that one child was missing. *Ach, mei,* what a poor substitute mother I am! Early this morning, before five o'clock, the van driver was ready to start for Wisconsin. He was startled "half out of his wits," he said, to see a head pop up from the backseat. Four-year-old Leona had spent the rest of the night sleeping in the van without waking, protected from the cold by her heavy coat and a blanket.

Blinking and bewildered, she had no idea of where she was, at first. The van driver tried to talk to her. But since she only knew Pennsylvania German and had not yet gone to school and learned English, she couldn't understand a word he said. She blinked back tears all the way home. He carried her into the house and knocked on the door.

I had just gotten up and was opening the draft on the stove and riddling down the ashes when I heard the knock. What a shock to see him there with Leona!

He said, "You have a brave little girl here. She must've had a guardian angel looking out for her."

Oh dear, I hope Betty won't find out about this. It would be too hard on her. *Ach, Yammerschtand!* (what a mess of trouble). I'm not fit to have the care of these children.

February 22
.... Again today there were loads and loads of laundry to do. There was a good brisk wind blowing, so it promised to be a good drying

day. There are four bed wetters in this household, which makes a lot of work and laundry.

Right after I'd sent the scholars off to school and washed the breakfast dishes, I headed swiftly up the stairs to gather the bedding and laundry. *Fui* (ugh)! I held my nose as I went into the children's room, wondering what Betty does about it.

Bed wetters! I opened a window for fresh air, when bang! a gust of wind slammed the door shut with such a crash that the knob fell off. Yes, it had been wobbly and in need of repair before, but now it was off. I tried to put the knob back on, but the stem had fallen out into the hallway. The door was soundly latched, as firmly as if locked. I tried every way I could think of to open that stubborn door, but nothing worked.

I became nearly frantic, thinking of those loads of laundry to be done. Down in the washhouse, the water was hot and waiting. Enos was planning to go to a sale at nine o'clock, and I feared I'd be locked up all day. I shouted until I was hoarse and pounded on the door until my hands were sore, but no one heard.

The preschoolers were alone in the kitchen, at the other end of the house. What mischief or danger would they get into? I felt awful about the situation. I went to the open window, but it faced to the back and not toward the barn. No use trying to holler for Enos. Then, looking down, I wondered, *Would it be safe to jump?*

If only there would be a roof or grape arbor there! After all, I had practice in shinnying down poles! But there was nothing to climb down, and I decided not to jump. Having my leg broken would be a lot worse than being trapped.

I found it hard to stay calm, so I prayed and sang a few songs. Then suddenly an idea struck me, and I jumped up. The bedsheets! I took two sheets and knotted the ends securely together. The chest of drawers held a good supply of sheets, more than I would need. I knotted more together to make a rope and tied one end to a bedpost. Then I climbed onto a windowsill and tried to summon the courage to let myself down.

I was shivering with apprehension, but finally I took a deep breath and a leap of faith and down I went! Thankfully, the knots held as I slid down. Utter gratitude flooded my heart when I safely reached the ground. Doing the laundry that day was a joy instead of a burden.

Since then, I've been pondering that happening and thinking backward with remorse and shame. I used to sneak out of my room via the grapevine pole. That was wrong, even though I now was able to use that climbing skill for a good purpose.

I know God forgives us our sins when we confess and repent of them. But we will still have to face the consequences of our misdeeds. I somberly wondered about what consequences I may yet have to face because of my headstrong selfishness. What would happen if Matthew found it out?

I'm afraid he would lose respect for me and never want to see me again. If only I could be sixteen again and start my *rumschpringing* years over, how differently I would act! But come what may, I must accept the consequences.

> God pity them both! And pity us all,
> Who vainly the dreams of youth recall;
> For of all sad words of tongue and pen,
> The saddest are these: "It might have been!"

March 2
....

Betty is home now but must have complete bed rest. Even so, things are going a bit better now that she's here. Enos was hungry for homemade cheese, so I tried my hand at cooking some. Only once before had I made any, and that was under Mamm's supervision. Betty gave me some instructions from the bedroom.

I had the thick, sour milk on the stove to scald at 120 degrees, or until it is too hot to hold a finger in it, since we have no food thermometer. Somehow or other, I managed to scorch it a bit. Oh no! There were little brown flecks floating around in it.

I felt like dumping the whole mess out into the pig's trough and having a good cry! But I drained the curds, mixed in the rest of the ingredients, and finished it in a double boiler. After it was molded, it looked real nice, except for the little brown bits.

At the dinner table, Enos took a chunk of it, tasted it, and a pleased but puzzled expression crossed his face. "What did you put in here?" he asked. "Did you put in bacon bits? Or herbs of some sort?"

"I don't give away my recipe secrets," I said, and I didn't tell him what happened.

March 29

March winds are howling today. It seems like I've been here at Enos's place for ages already, though it's actually not quite two months yet. I've found out one thing since I'm here— why mothers get gray!

This afternoon I looked out the window into the barnyard and saw seven-year-old Neil standing on the peak of the *Heisli* (outhouse) roof. He was holding the big black buggy umbrella open above him. Then he took a flying leap off it and fell flat on his face as he hit the ground. Oh no!

I ran out in a panic to pick up the pieces, expecting to find him with more than one broken bone. But by the time I got there, he was up, seemingly unhurt, and muttering to himself about the stupid umbrella not working right. Eventually I pumped the rest of the story out of him.

At school Neil saw a picture of a parachutist floating to the ground, and he had a brainstorm. Why not make his own parachute so he could fly, too! Then he got the bright idea of using the big buggy umbrella, climbing to the top of the windmill, and jumping off with it.

He said he took the umbrella and climbed the rungs up to the top of the windmill, stood on the platform there, opened the umbrella, and prepared to jump. He was even thinking of calling me to come outside and watch him glide to earth.

Oh my! I'm so glad I didn't see him at that stage, just before he was ready to sail. I'd have been a nervous wreck! He looked down to the ground and saw his pet puppy looking up at him, sitting right at the spot where he was planning to land. Fearing he would thump down on the puppy and hurt him, Neil climbed back down and put the puppy into the safety of the barn.

That was when he got the notion of testing his idea from the roof of the *Heisli*. That puppy may well have saved Neil's life. I believe he had a guardian angel looking out for him, too, as the van driver said. I just hope these children will all be kept safe somehow or other until I leave here.

Looking forward to my dates with Matthew on Sunday evenings is what keeps me going all week. Ah, sweet love, that makes my burden light!

Stresses and Strains

April 15

Warm, scented breezes are making the laundry on the line snap and flap with glee. Yet poor Betty can't be out to enjoy this lovely spring weather. She hasn't been well at all, and now she's back in the hospital for more tests. Enos goes in to see her every day. So the boys have to struggle at doing the chores the best they can.

Enos Jr. stepped or jumped onto a rusty nail, and it went all the way through his shoe sole and sock, and deep into his foot. This morning his foot was all swollen and red and draining pus. I thought he should see a doctor, but dad Enos told me how to doctor it at home. "Soak it in hot comfrey tea and cream of tartar water four times a day. Then put on a poultice of homemade salve with bread soaked in milk, and bandage it." Oh dear! I'm so worried that he'll get lockjaw!

Then last night Uria forgot to close the gate to the driving horse's stall. The horse spent the night eating all the grain and hay he wanted. This morning he was bloated, sick, and obviously miserable. Enos had already left, so I told Dannie to lead him back and forth from one end of the feedlot to the other. We hoped that might save him, as it once had saved one of my dad's horses.

Dannie kept it up for an hour, and then the horse suddenly fell over dead. What a sight for Enos when he came home from the hospital, to find his good road horse lying there dead! He was disgusted about it and curtly told me I should have had the boys tie the foundered horse in a shallow part of the creek, to keep his feet cool.

I was tense and wound up and bawled as I put the never-ending loads of laundry through the wringer. I thought, *Do I really want to get married?* Yes, I know Enos has plenty of troubles just now, but couldn't he see what a strain I am under here, caring for his family? Oh, to be back home with Mamm and Daed, free from all care and responsibility!

April 17
.... Enos Jr.'s foot looked a lot better this morning, and that was a load off my mind! I guess dad Enos knew what he was doing after all, or else God performed a miracle.

Betty sent a note home with Enos, saying, "It's time to plant the one kind of peas. They are in a labeled glass jar on the *Kesselhaus* (kettle-house) shelf. Please take good care of them because they are from heirloom seed stock, handed down by my great-grandmother. I save seed from each year's crop because that kind is not available in any store."

So after the usual morning rush, I took my hoe and the seeds and headed for the garden. Enos had nicely prepared the soil so it was as fit as could be. I began to make the rows. Five-year-old Atlee was with me and wanted to help. I told him that as soon as I'd made all the rows, he could help to drop the seeds into the furrows.

He stood waiting for a while with the open jar, then ran off to play with the puppy until I would be ready. I was just finished making the last furrow when I heard a yelp from Atlee. "Hey, the roosters are eating the pea seeds!"

Sure enough, two big Golden Cross roosters had overturned the jar and were gobbling the seeds as fast as they could. With sinking heart, I raised my hoe and made a dash for the roosters. They ran for safety under the *Kesselhaus* porch, but it was too late. Only a few seeds remained—Betty's precious heir-loom seeds!

I stood stunned for a few moments. Then I decided those roosters shall lose their heads, and fast! I told Atlee, "Stand guard at the porch so the roosters don't run off." Then I ran to the shop for the hatchet. I crawled under the porch myself, wriggling on my belly until I had cornered the roosters and grabbed a leg of each one.

I knew I would have to act quickly, before the peas were out of their gullets and at the mercy of digestive juices. I thought, *Oh dear, now what shall I do with the one rooster until I've beheaded the other?* I knew Atlee wasn't strong enough to hold it. Then I had a bright idea—in the *Heisli!* I made sure the lids were shut, threw the rooster inside, and made Atlee hold the door shut.

Then off to the chopping block I went. Whack! Whack! One was done. Old Smarty in the outhouse nearly got away for me when I opened the privy door, but I managed to grab him by the tail. In a few minutes his fate was sealed, too.

Atlee kept asking over and over, "How can they see to jump around so without a head?"

There was no time for me to answer. I ran to the kitchen for the butcher knife, cut open the first rooster's gullet, and retrieved the precious seeds. I put them back in the jar and quickly ran to the pump to wash them. Then I did the same with the second rooster. What a relief when I finally had all the heirloom seeds safely planted, covered with ground! Now, if only they come up and thrive.

I heated water and worked hard to butcher those big roosters. We had a scrumptious fried chicken supper.

Enos asked me, "What gave you the notion to butcher those roosters today? I would have chopped off their heads for you if you would have asked."

I was saved from answering when Marie piped up, "I'm so glad they're gone. Now Leona and I won't have to be afraid to go to the *Heisli* anymore when the roosters are near." I hope Atlee doesn't tell.

Betty is coming home tomorrow. I don't think I'll sleep well until I see those pea plants peeking through the ground.

I've been having envious thoughts of Becky Yoder as Birch Hollow schoolmarm, with the happy end-of-year school activities. There are the board meetings, maybe a surprise lunch, the lessons, and the closing picnic. Meanwhile, I struggle here with endless responsibilities, loads and loads of laundry and dirty diapers, all the other work, and all kinds of trials besides.

Enos and Betty had to head back to the hospital this morning for yet another round of tests. I spent the morning in the garden, doing more planting, and felt gloriously happy when I saw that the heirloom peas are coming up in neat rows.

My happiness was shattered, though, when in midmorning Atlee came dashing out the *Kesselhaus* door, crying, "Dora, oh, Dora, come quick. There's something awfully wrong with Marie." Choking down panic, I dropped everything and ran, not knowing what terrible thing to expect.

In the kitchen I found three-year-old Marie staggering around, laughing loudly, staggering some more, and saying funny, senseless things. I never saw anyone who was drunk. But from what I've heard and read, it fit the description.

"*Was is letz? Bisht du narrisch?* (what's wrong? are you crazy?)" Leona kept asking.

Atlee came with an empty bottle and thrust it at me, with a scared look on his face. He said, "Marie drank this. Do you think she'll die?"

I read the label. Oh no! Poison ivy lotion! Dannie

had gone to the drugstore last night for something for Uria's bad case of poison ivy. She must have drunk the full bottle.

"What shall I do?" I wondered aloud. We don't have a telephone. What a helpless feeling! I would have to go to the neighbors' place, and the nearest one wasn't close. Then I thought of Mrs. Morris, who gets her milk here at the farm and lives about a half mile away. Hadn't she said that she was a nurse?

Quickly I got the children's wagon and put Marie and the empty bottle in it. I slipped a pillow under her head and used a leather strap to fasten the happy-go-lucky little girl down, to keep her from rolling off the wagon. I ordered Atlee to stay with Leona and little Katie and take care of them. Then I hurried off, wondering for the hundredth time why I had ever agreed to take this job.

What if Mrs. Morris wasn't at home? What if the children at home would find the matches and set fire to the place? All kinds of terrible thoughts plagued me. What if Marie died before I got there? It seemed like ages till I finally reached her home. What a relief it was to have the kind-faced old lady come to the door. I handed the empty bottle and the drunk little girl over to her and told her my tale of woe.

Mrs. Morris quickly called the poison control center and got the necessary information. She told me, "The lotion is mostly alcohol, and the other ingredients aren't going to harm Marie. As for the alcohol, it will just take time for it to get out of her system."

Oh, what a relief! Marie fell asleep on the way home and slept till after supper. Then she was her usual self again. But I still feel all wound up, jittery, and unable to relax. I wish I'd be at home with Mamm and Daed. I think I have a bad case of *Heemweh*.

May 6

Matthew came for me tonight to take me to the singing, but he seemed rather remote and silent, not at all like his usual, friendly self. "Is something bothering you?" I asked.

He shrugged it off and gave me an evasive answer. Matthew didn't have much to say on the way home either. After awhile, I gave up trying to make conversation, thinking, *Two can play at this game.*

Matthew dropped me off at the end of Enos's lane, without bringing me in to the house. He merely said, "See you next Sunday," and left.

What, oh what, could have happened to make him so half-hearted? I'm so tired and discouraged tonight. I've been thinking this over so much that my tired brain can no longer think straight. Is this the beginning of the end?

I guess that Matthew has found out about my disobedience in sneaking out with Gideon, and that leaves him cold. If so, I might as well accept the fact that it's all over between us. I'm reaping what I sowed.

We've all come down with yet another case of stomach flu, similar to the first week I was here. *Ach, Elend* (oh, misery), I feel like a wrung-out dishrag. All those mounds of laundry are always staring me in the face, all those dirty dishes, and I'm so tired, tired, tired. All I want to do is soak in a tub of warm water, and then crawl into bed and sleep for a week.

First, I have a letter to write—to Matthew. Yesterday, on our in-between Sunday (no services), we were out for a drive together. Again he was so quiet and closed into himself. By the time he brought me back, I was completely discouraged.

I've changed my mind about marriage. Courtship leads to marriage, and I've decided that I'll never get married. I don't even care if Matthew doesn't want me anymore. After being here at Enos' and seeing how raising a family can go, well, I think I've made up my mind. I'll make teaching school my lifework. It's a noble and worthy profession.

Year after year, I could be a good influence on my pupils and an example to them. I would influence them for the good and direct them into paths of uprightness. If Matthew thinks I am not trustworthy, well—I could never marry a man who has no respect for me, anyway.

Ya well, I'm so bone weary, and I haven't been able to think straight for the last several days. But I will write that letter to Matthew yet before I collapse. Then I'll have the soaking bath, and please, God, let me sleep uninterrupted for as long as I wish. Amen.

Oh yes, tomorrow I must tell Enos that he has to find another *Maad* (hired girl). I'm going home to Mamm and Daed as soon as I can find a van going to Pennsylvania.

May 18

We had a refreshing rain today. Betty's twenty-one-year-old sister, Verna, and her husband arrived from Missouri to stay for a week. The doctors have found Betty's problem. With the proper medication and treatment, she should soon be on the mend. I am feeling much better, too, and can think straight again.

I've decided that on Sunday evening at the singing, I'll talk to Matthew and tell him all about Gideon and me and that it wasn't as bad as it might have sounded. I'll tell him to disregard my poor letter. *Ach mei!* Why did I ever send it? I was so blue and discouraged, and I didn't mean a word I wrote. How could I have been such a *Dummkopp* (blockhead)?

I wish I could go and talk to Matthew right now. But of course I can't, not unless I'd hitch up Enos's new road horse that he has on trial and is thinking of sending back. He balked for Enos when he drove him the first time on Tuesday, and he acted ornery at a crossing.

Sigh! I guess I'll be sitting on pins and needles until Sunday night, when I'll get to talk with

Matthew so everything will be all right between us again. I can hardly get over it that I sent that letter. Of all the stupid things to do!

May 19

It's all over now, and there's an unbearable ache in my heart. Enos went to the Amish bulk food store this forenoon and came home with the distressing news that Matthew is leaving. He's heading west for the summer, to work on a produce farm in California, and he's going by train. Oh no!

Enos had tied his still-harnessed horse under the barn forebay, intending to use him again before unhitching. I ran out the door with a sense of great urgency, without thinking twice about what I was doing or even putting on my bonnet. I untied the horse, grabbed the reins, and jumped on the buggy. The whip was in the socket, and I urged the horse to go faster and faster. I thought I just had to get there before Matthew left.

Five miles to go. "If only it were closer," I lamented in anguish. Bits of mud and gravel were flying into my face, and we careened crazily around a corner. At the next crossroad, I didn't slacken the horse's pace, for I could see that nothing was coming. Soon the horse began to slow down. I tapped him with the whip to speed him up again, but he angrily lashed his tail from side to side and refused to speed up.

I had to stop at the highway for a car, and then the stubborn beast refused to budge again. I tapped him sharply with the whip, but to no avail. Then in tearful impatience, I tapped him even harder. Wham! He kicked back against the mud flap. I had an urge to jump off and leave the stupid critter and run the rest of the way, when along came Junior Miller on a scooter. He came to a stop, with questions in his eyes.

"My horse is balking," I said, close to tears. "Can you do something to start him?"

Junior obligingly tried to lead him, but the horse only shook his head angrily and planted his feet more firmly on the ground. That was when I hatched a bright idea. "Blow in his ears," I suggested. "That's supposed to start off a balker."

"Well, I guess I could try it," Junior drawled. Ever so slowly, he blew in the horse's ear.

I wanted to shout, "Hurry, hurry, not so slow." It did work. The horse took off, fast enough to suit even me in my frenzy. The scenery whizzed by. At last I spied the Bontrager farm buildings up ahead. We rounded the last curve on two wheels and pulled up to the barn in a flurry of flying gravel.

Hurriedly, with trembling hands, I tied the horse to the ring beside the barn. I was thinking, *Oh, if only he's here yet, and we can talk, and everything will be all right again.* But it was not to be.

Rosabeth came running out of the house, and when I saw her tear-stained face, I knew I was too late.

"Matthew left," she said sadly, blowing her nose. "Gone to California to work for a produce farmer he met when he was in Kansas. The man has a thousand acres, and he offered Matthew a job."

"When is he coming back?" I managed to choke out.

Rosabeth shook her head. "He didn't say. I can't understand it. Mamm and Daed didn't want him to go, but he told them not to worry about him, and that he would be back sometime."

"Don't you have an address or phone number, so I could write to him or call him?" I asked sadly, not expecting her to have one.

"Oh yes, an address. I'll get it for you." Rosabeth went to the house and came back with a slip of paper. There was no phone number, only the name of the produce farm and the address.

There was nothing else for me to do but go back. Having his address was a small consolation. Maybe if I write to him, after a week or two, his wanderlust will be settled, and he will come back.

On the way home, I noticed that a lilac bush on a south slope was blooming. I was overwhelmed with a great sadness, thinking of last year at lilac time, how Matthew had adorned his horse with lilac blossoms, and how happy we were. I don't think I could bear it if I didn't have a small hope that if I write to him, he will come right back.

June 6
.... I'm back at home with Mamm, Daed, Peter, Sadie, and Crist, hoping that in the comfort of their love and kindness, my wounded heart

will slowly begin to heal. But I know that no matter how lighthearted and carefree I appear to others, deep inside there is a pocket of pain that will never go away until Matthew is safely home.

I wrote a letter to him the very day of my wild race and told him everything. I explained that I'm going home but that I'm longing to hear from him.

Each day, since I'm home, when it's mail time, I hover in sight of the mailbox until the carrier goes by. Then I check the box and come away, choking back disappointment.

I feel so restless. Maybe God will help me if I pray with my *Prayer Book for Earnest Christians:*

The waves of affliction slam against my little ship, and it seems about to sink. So from the depths of my soul, I call to you, O God! with genuine grief, just as Jairus called to you for his little daughter. Oh, come to me with help before I sink in deep depression.

That prayer certainly echoes my feelings. I'm not the only one struggling against depression and crying out to God.

Here is another verse that fits my despair:

Therefore, I pray even more, have mercy on me. Console me, O Lord! in my distress. Since you are so merciful, I pray with Mary Magdalene: O Lord! see, like that impure woman, I am sorely afraid and in need of help. And I ask, help me, weak as I am. If I could only touch the hem of your garment, I would be made whole.

Oh, I implore God to keep Matthew safe, even though he is so far away from home, and away from the godly influence of his parents and the church.

July 5

I just put yet another letter in the mail for Matthew. As yet I have received no answer to the four that I have already sent him. This is the last one I'm sending. I'm giving up now. His heart must be hardened toward me, and his mind made up.

I've begged him to just send me a few lines, at least, and tell me how he feels. But I guess he doesn't count it worth the time and postage. I've written to Rosabeth, and she wrote back, saying she can't understand it at all, since he's written several letters to them.

She says Matthew is busy helping to harvest the produce on the farm and says he has a good job lined up for fall and winter, too. That news saddened them since they were so hoping he would be home by fall. He travels to church services at a new Amish settlement in the hills about ten miles from his farm. It is quite an encouragement to hear that he is not abandoning his faith.

Yes, I guess I must accept the fact that Matthew just doesn't want me anymore. I must give up my will and say to God, "Not my will, but Thine be done." I'll just have to trust that God's grace will be sufficient for me.

I've been helping here at home this summer, doing whatever I had the ambition to do, but that wasn't much. But I must find myself another job to occupy my mind and interests. I can't go on brooding forever.

I'll just have to be that wayside flower that does something useful. I must put my past mistakes and failures behind me and press forward toward the prize of the high calling of God.

"Godliness with contentment is great gain" and leads to *Gelassenheit* (submission to God). I must give up my self-will and yield myself to God's work in my life.

The purple martins are doing their best to impart cheer to me, with their musical warbling and chirping. Sadie and Crist are taking turns cranking, making homemade ice cream with crushed ice from town for Grandpa Daves. Henrys and Rudys are also coming for supper. I still have plenty of blessings, more than I deserve. I choose not to be gloomy.

July 23

I had a frightening dream last night—or rather, two dreams. First, I dreamed that Matthew was riding a motorcycle. As I watched, he began to career crazily from side to side, then crashed into a telephone pole. I started to run toward him to see if he was hurt. When I got closer, Matthew stood up, and I saw to my horror that his one leg was missing.

That dream faded away. Then I saw him driving a snowmobile through a snowy field. Up over the horizon came another snowmobile and crashed into him, and I knew that Matthew was killed. I tried to scream, but no sound came out.

Then I awoke. Oh, what a relief to know that it was only a dream. I so much want Matthew to come back, safe and sound, even though he won't come back to *me*. As long as he is all right and not led astray, that's all I pray for now.

As for my life, I keep thinking of the saying, "Let another's shipwreck be your beacon." I hope that if anyone has found out about my youthful rebellion, they will take a lesson from it. I was sowing wild oats. Though I pulled out the wild stuff and now want to plant good seed, I must still bear the consequences.

August 1
.... A letter came from Isaac Bontragers. They're wondering if I will consent to be the Birch Hollow schoolmarm again this year. No wonder Becky Yoder asked to finish the term last year. She probably suspected or knew she'd be getting married this fall and wouldn't have the chance to teach again.

So now I have a decision to make. Do I want to

go back to all those memories of Matthew? Would I be able to stand it? In that fateful letter, I told Matthew that I wanted to dedicate my life to teaching school. Now that I have the opportunity, will I let it slip by?

I'll pray about it and talk it over with Mamm and Daed. If I do teach, I must get busy, for there will be a lot to do to get ready. Not much time for journal writing.

September 2

Here I am, back in my cozy little *Daadihaus* at Mahlon Swartzentruber's place. I arrived on Friday and spent yesterday at the school, organizing things. Tomorrow is the first day of school at Birch Hollow. Today is the in-between Sunday (no church services), so I had a chance to visit with Mahlons and go for a walk.

This neighborhood brought back a flood of memories, now so bittersweet and filled with heartaches, for Matthew isn't here. I was wondering how I was going to be able to keep my spirits up tonight. Then Rosabeth came with a group of jolly, laughing, and chattering girls.

We had a merry evening after all, renewing friendships and catching up on the community news. Now I simply must go to bed if I want to teach tomorrow.

October 5

"October's bright blue weather." There's little time for journal writing. Mahlon's wife, Lydia, in the other part of the house, broke her wrist. Now I spend my evenings helping them out. It does me good to keep so busy.

School is going well. I have eighteen pupils this year, and I am in earnest about being a good example to them, as well as a good teacher. The sweet innocent faces of the little first-graders looking up at me make me aware of the awesome responsibility that is mine.

Their personalities and characters are still pliable, like pieces of clay in a potter's hand, and can still be shaped. But once they're grown, the clay will be hardened. I hope I am worthy of the parents' trust.

November 22

Thanksgiving Day. I was invited to Isaac and Rosemary's for dinner. All the time I was there, I was aware of the undercurrent of sadness. How much they miss Matthew!

A fresh wave of guilt nearly overwhelmed me as I wondered how much I had to do with his departure. Isaacs have good hope that he will return with the same character he had when he left. But they can't be sure. As long as he's not back, there's that fear.

When I came home, I had a fit of crying, face down on the bed. I hope Mahlons did not hear me.

December 26

Christmas Day passed with no word from Matthew. I have an awful case of *Heemweh* tonight, thinking of the family and friends gathering and feasting today at home, on this Second Christmas.

Mahlon Lydia invited me for dinner. She had invited some newlyweds. Seeing those happy couples sent a pang of sadness into my heart, thinking of Matthew celebrating Christmas so far from home.

I think maybe I should try once more to write him a letter. But I don't have his address here. I must have left it at home. No, on second thought, I guess I won't write. If he had wanted to, he'd have answered my other letters.

February 10

Dear diary, you are being sadly neglected of late, and it's just as well, for you have so few empty pages left. School was getting to be somewhat monotonous this last while until several of the parents came up with a few day-brighteners.

Last week one day, we received the word, "No packed lunches tomorrow." Junior Millers had planned a treasure hunt for the scholars, with notes for us in different mailboxes.

One said, "Sing three songs for old Mrs. Kreider, then look in her mailbox," and so on. During several more stops, we were singing more songs and getting hungrier and hungrier. Finally we ended in the kitchen at the Millers. We had a delicious feast, which gave us energy for the cold, snowy tramp back to school.

On Thursday the scholars had a fruit roll planned for me. In the midst of our geography lesson, Johnnie all of a sudden began to clap his hands loudly. The apples, oranges, grapefruits, tin cans, and snacks came rolling up front. I was amazed that they managed to keep it such a secret! I filled a big box with all the goodies. Now I guess I'll have to share some with the neighbors.

March 29

I thought and thought, but thought in vain.
At last I thought I'd sign my name.

That old autograph verse expresses my feelings when it comes to making a decision on whether or not I should try writing to Matthew again. If I write, *what* should I write? Should I or should I not? "To be, or not to be" writing: "that is the question." Something inside is urging me to write, and yet I don't want to keep on throwing myself at Matthew if he's not interested.

It's such a nice spring evening. I think I'll walk over to visit Rosabeth and see what she says. If she thinks I should write, she can give me Matthew's address again. At least the walk will do me good.

April 10

My twentieth birthday. I received a flat, wrapped package from Mamm in the mail—another brand-new journal, and a birthday greeting card. I guess I must've mentioned to her that my old one was nearly full. Do I want to start another journal? I'm not sure yet.

I'll be watching the mail closely again soon. I finally worked up the courage to try writing to Matthew once more. Rosabeth thought I should, and she gave me his address. I wrote him a letter every evening for a whole week, but tore each one to bits again and chucked them into the stove the next morning. Finally yesterday I vowed to send one, and I did, for better or for worse.

April 25

I have come to the last page of my journal, and I have something important and amazing to record. At last I received a letter from Matthew! I still can hardly believe it. My heart is overflowing with emotions, and I don't know whether I should rejoice or weep.

Yesterday when I came home from school, I found his letter in the mail. With trembling fingers and thumping heart, I opened it. I could have cried an ocean of tears. He wrote that he had never received any of the earlier letters I had sent him in California! I guess I had the wrong zip code or something.

Anyway, all that time he thought I still felt the same as I did when I wrote that fateful letter just before he left Minnesota. He wrote that he's coming home for a visit as soon as he can get away, probably around lilac blossom time.

Back for a *visit?* What does he mean? Isn't he coming home to stay? These questions put a noose of fear around my heart. Has Matthew changed a lot? His letter reveals nothing of his feelings. Has he found another girl out there, wherever he is, maybe one that's not of our faith?

The fact that he wrote "at lilac blossom time" gives me a ray of hope that maybe he still cares for me. Or maybe he himself doesn't know for sure and is still undecided.

Oh, I hope those lilacs hurry up and bloom. I'm afraid I won't rest well until he gets here and I know what's in his heart. For a long time last night, I was too excited to sleep.

When I finally did fall asleep after two o'clock, I dreamed that Matthew was here, walking in the lane toward me, smiling, his arms loaded with lilac blossoms. I ran out to meet him. But when he saw me, he dropped the lilacs and vanished into thin air.

Maybe God is preparing me to realize that Matthew and I aren't meant for each other after all. I must pray for God's will to be done and for grace to cheerfully submit to his leading. I keep telling myself that all I ask of God now is that Matthew will be as dear and unspoiled as he was when we first met, as pure in heart, and as fervent in serving the Lord.

If he has backslidden in any way, I pray that he will be fully restored. If God has someone else planned for him, I resolve still to rejoice and be grateful. I vow that not a word of complaint shall cross my lips, nor a trace of bitterness or jealousy lodge in my heart.

I will finish this journal with a prayer from my *Prayer Book:*

O holy, dear Father, reigning in your kingdom! We thank you once more and indeed offer you what you deserve, our greatest praise, honor, and glory.

We declare our manifold and deepest thanks for all your unspeakably glorious goodness and acts of mercy, for all your blessings, spiritual and temporal gifts of grace, and deeds of kindness which cannot be counted. . . .

We especially thank you for your eternal salvation, which you have presented to us in Christ Jesus our Lord. . . .

Oh! holy God and Father! help us and make us able to conduct ourselves daily in your fear and to your holy honor. . . .

Thy kingdom come.
Thy will be done on earth,
      as it is in heaven.

Amen.

Rules for Teachers

1872

1. Teachers each day will fill lamps and clean chimneys.
2. Each teacher will bring a bucket of water and a scuttle of coal for the day's session.
3. Make your pens carefully. You may whittle nibs to the individual taste of the pupils.
4. Men teachers may take one evening each week for courting purposes, or two evenings a week if they go to church regularly.
5. After ten hours in school, teachers may spend the remaining time reading the Bible or other good books.
6. Women teachers who marry or engage in unseemly conduct will be dismissed.
7. Every teacher should lay aside from each pay a goodly sum of earnings for a benefit during declining years, so as not to become a burden on society.
8. Any teacher who smokes, uses liquor in any form, frequents pool or public halls, or gets shaved in a barbershop will give good reason for parents to suspect his worth, intention, integrity, and honesty.

1915

1. You will not marry during the term of your contract.
2. You are not to keep company with men.
3. You must be home between the hours of 8:00 p.m. and 6:00 a.m. unless attending a school function.
4. You may not loiter downtown in ice-cream stores.

5. You may not travel beyond the city limits unless you have the permission of the chairman of the board.
6. You may not ride alone in a carriage or automobile with any man unless he is your father or brother.
7. You may not smoke cigarettes.
8. You may not dress in bright colors.
9. You may under no circumstances dye your hair.
10. You must wear at least two petticoats.
11. Your dresses may not be any shorter than two inches above the ankles.
12. To keep the schoolroom neat and clean, you must sweep the floor at least once daily; scrub the floor at least once a week with hot soapy water; clean the blackboards at least once a day; and start the fire at 7:00 a.m. so the room will be warm by 8:00 a.m.

Rules for Schoolchildren

1760s

1. Dear child, when you enter the school, bow respectfully and take your place quietly, thinking of the presence of God.
2. During prayers, and at the mention of God's Word, remember that God speaks with you, and be reverent and attentive.
3. If you are called upon to pray aloud, speak slowly and thoughtfully, and in singing do not try to outscream the others or have the first word.
4. Always be obedient to your teacher and do not cause him to remind you of the same thing many times.
5. If you are punished for your naughtiness, do not express impatience in words or manner, but accept your punishment for your improvement.
6. At school avoid scandalous talking, by which you make your teacher's work more difficult, annoy other pupils, and disturb the attention of yourself and others.
7. Attend to all that is told, sit up straight, and look at your teacher.
8. If you are to recite your lesson, open your book without noise, read loudly, slowly, and distinctly, that every word and syllable may be understood.
9. Attend more to yourself than to others unless you are appointed monitor.
10. If you are not asked, keep quiet and do not prompt others. Let them speak and answer for themselves.
11. Toward your fellows act lovingly and peacefully; do

not quarrel with them, hit them, dirty their clothes with your shoes or ink, nor give them nicknames. Act toward them always as you would have them act toward you.

12. Avoid all improper, vulgar habits or actions at school, such as (1) stretching with laziness the hands or the whole body; (2) eating fruit or other things in school; (3) leaning one's hand or arm on a neighbor's shoulder, leaning the head on the hand, or laying it on the desk; (4) putting one's feet on the bench or letting them dangle or scrape, crossing the legs or spreading them too far apart in sitting or standing; (5) scratching the head; (6) playing with the fingers or chewing them; (7) turning the head in all directions; (8) sitting and sleeping; (9) crawling under benches or desks; (10) turning the back upon the teacher; (11) changing one's clothes in school; (12) acting indecently in school.

13. Keep your books clean inside and out; do not scribble or draw in them; do not lose or tear them.

14. In writing, do not soil your hands and face with ink, and do not spatter the ink on the desk or on the clothes of yourself or other children.

15. When school is out, do not make a clatter. In going down stairs, do not jump two or three steps at a time, lest you hurt yourself. Go quietly home.

Credits

Dreams and Schemes

April 10: 1 Samuel 16:7; Proverbs 31:30.

April 13: Proverbs 31:28.

April 21: Matthew 19:14.

May 6: Matthew 19:17.

June 18: James Russell Lowell, "What is so rare?" John Heywood, "All is well that ends well."

February 12: Proverbs 16:18.

February 20: Deuteronomy 21:18-21; Luke 10:13-14; 18:13.

March 14: Ecclesiastes 1:2, 14.

March 24: *Prayer Book for Earnest Christians*, trans. and ed. by Leonard Gross, from *Die ernsthafte Christenpflicht* [1708] (Scottdale, Pa.: Herald Press, 1997), 1.

Nursemaid and Teacher

April 10: John Greenleaf Whittier, in "Maud Muller," stanza 53; Augusta J. Evans-Wilson, *St. Elmo* (New York: A. L. Burt Co., n.d.).

May 9: 1 Corinthians 1:30; Revelation 1:5.

May 19: Acts 1:1-11; Proverbs 13:15.

June 17: 1 Thessalonians 5:22; *Prayer Book*, 125-126.

July 1: The eighteen articles are the Dordrecht Confession of Faith, 1632, as in van Braght's *Martyrs Mirror*, 3d English ed., trans. by J. F. Sohm from original Dutch ed. of 1660 (Scottdale, Pa.: Herald Press, 1938), 38-44; Matthew 5:6; Charlotte Elliott, "Just as I Am."

July 8: Proverbs 3:4-6.

August 25: Matthew 6:33; John 1:12; Revelation 1:5.

September 18: Thomas à Kempis, *Of the Imitation of Christ*

(New York: Hurst & Co., n.d.), 200 (4.9.2); 1 Peter 5:7.
October 29: Luke 9:62; 2 Corinthians 12:9.
October 31: Psalm 121:1-2; author unknown, "I'm queen."
November 6: Matthew 5:46; 6:12-15; 18:21-22; Romans 4:18; Matthew 5:48.
December 5: Isaiah 55:8-9; William Cowper, "God moves," adapted.
February 14: Isaiah 43:25.
March 26: Matthew 7:12, Golden Rule; Whittier.

Lilacs and Love
September 5: Philippians 4:8.
October 7: Proverbs 6:6.
February 17: Psalm 34:7; 91:11; Matthew 18:10, angel.
February 22: Whittier.
March 29: Matthew 11:30.

Stresses and Strains
June 6: *Prayer Book*, 90-91; Mark 5:22-43; Luke 8:2.
July 5: Luke 22:42; 2 Corinthians 12:9; Philippians 3:14; 1 Timothy 6:6.
October 5: Helen Hunt Jackson, "October's . . . weather."
March 29: Shakespeare, in *Hamlet*, "To be or not to be."
April 25: *Prayer Book*, 48-49, 132.

Rules for Teachers
Not all these rules, reworded slightly, apply in Amish communities, but they tell readers about old customs. Becky Yoder did quit teaching school before her marriage. Yet while teaching, Dora could have dates with Matthew. Pupils are recruited to help with routine cleaning duties or with drilling younger students. Rules of 1872: source unknown. Rules of 1915: *Convention Herald*.

Rules for Schoolchildren

Christopher Dock, Colonial Schoolmaster: The Biography and Writings of Christopher Dock, by Gerald C. Studer (Scottdale, Pa.: Herald Press, 1967, 1993), 343-345; used by permission.

The Author

The author's pen name is Carrie Bender. She is a member of an old order group. With her husband and children, she lives among the Amish in Lancaster County, Pennsylvania.